About the Author

Sue was born in London, brought up by her grandmother in the south of England, and then served as a police officer in Hampshire for many years, before retiring and moving to Yorkshire where she became a shepherd in the Yorkshire Dales. She has sung in operatic societies and choirs all her life. She now lives in the Yorkshire Wolds, and writes a weekly diary for a regional paper, and cares for her three dogs, and an elderly cat.

To Sit in Solemn Silence

Sue Woodcock

To Sit in Solemn Silence

Pegasus

A CIP catalogue record for this title is
available from the British Library

ISBN: 978-1-910903 29-2

*Pegasus is an imprint of
Pegasus Elliot MacKenzie Publishers Ltd.*
www.pegasuspublishers.com

First Published in 2019

**Pegasus
Sheraton House Castle Park
Cambridge CB3 0AX England**

Printed & Bound in Great Britain

Dedication

To my friends, Julie and Mark, and to Susan Currier of the Celebration Singers in Pocklington, who has got me back into amateur operatics.

Chapter One

Saul Catchpole sat down in his seat just as the lights dimmed for the start of the operetta. He had taken his wife and two daughters to the first night of a performance of The Mikado. It was not really quite his cup of tea but he had noticed a flyer for it in his Murder Squad general office and had asked one of his detective sergeants, Geoff Bickerstaff, about it.

Geoff had admitted to putting up the flyer and that he was a member of the Amateur Operatic Society that was putting it on. Geoff also informed Saul that another member of the Murder Squad, Julia Pellow, was singing a principal part, and that some of Geoff's family were involved. Saul was not surprised about Geoff and his family but was very surprised that Julia was. He almost felt a duty to go and see the show and decided that it would be good for his two daughters, Susan and Sharon, to listen to something other than the latest pop idols. His wife Anna was quite happy to go, and they had arrived in plenty of time. They had indulged in a pre-opening drink and then went into the auditorium of the rather fine theatre and found their seats. Saul was the first to admit he was not a singer, in fact he couldn't sing at all, but he knew his daughter Sharon could and was in her school choir.

The production was very good, and Saul was able to relax as he followed the story and for the first time for a while, he managed to put aside his other worries and responsibilities.

When Julia Pellow came on and started to sing, Saul was very impressed. She was rather a retiring person at work and a conscientious and clever officer, but he had never pictured her as a diva but on this occasion, he saw a totally new side to her. Her portrayal of Petti-Sing was splendid, and he thought he should find out a little more about some of his team at work.

When Geoff Bickerstaff came on as Pooh-Bar Saul was equally impressed but not that surprised. Geoff had been a sergeant in the Murder Squad with Saul for some years and he was a totally reliable and good officer. At the interval they went up to the bar and Saul purchased soft drinks for the two girls. He and Anna had a glass of wine each.

Susan asked rather sarcastically, "You actually like this stuff, Dad? The cast are all ancient and it is a bit bizarre, don't you think?"

Saul grinned and said, "Yes I know but it is just a bit of fun. I think your mother and Sharon are enjoying it, so don't spoil it for them, eh? What would you rather be watching?"

"If you must know, Dad, The Fall."

Saul looked down at her and asked, "Who are they?"

Susan grinned and said, "I didn't think you would know. They are a punk group, and before you ask, I know you have heard of punk."

"Is that the noise you play in your room sometimes? Yes, I heard them, each to their own I suppose. Be a good girl don't spoil the rest of this for your mother and sister."

"Oh, OK, Dad, but you do need to get into this century you know. Just promise me I don't have to come to this kind of thing again."

Saul allowed himself a mischievous grin and said, "That would depend on how good your school reports are next term, wouldn't it?"

"That's blackmail, Dad, and you know it."

"Yes, but I also mean it. Come on let's get back to our seats that is the five-minute warning bell."

As they moved back to the auditorium Sharon said, "Dad, this is great, can I come to something else like this with you again? Even better would you mind if I joined a society like this? Do they have junior members?"

Saul was rather taken aback and said, "Let's find out, shall we? No, I wouldn't mind at all. Mind you, your school work must not suffer."

"Don't worry, Dad, it won't."

Saul glanced over at his wife and saw her smile and she surreptitiously nodded at him.

***

The second act was just as good, and Saul listened with great amusement to The Mikado's rendering of 'My Object All Sublime'. When the female Katisha was singing and acting Saul felt a severe chill run down his spine at her realistic viciousness, as she cackled, and he thought she must be a fine actress, either that or rather unpleasant in reality. The applause at the end was deafening and soon the lights came up and they filed out with the rest of the audience into the foyer.

One of the ushers approached him and said, "Mr Catchpole, sir, you and your family are invited backstage to meet the cast, some of whom I believe you already know. Would you like to come?"

Anna nodded briefly, and Susan gave a look of sheer exasperation, but Sharon said, "Can we, Dad, please?"

They were led backstage to what Saul realized was the Green Room where the cast were gathering. Geoff came over and said, "Did you enjoy it, sir?"

Saul said, "Here you call me Saul, Geoff, and yes I did. One of my daughters was most impressed and wants to know if you have a junior section because she is interested in joining."

Geoff, still covered in grotesque make-up, smiled and said, "Yes, actually we do. Can I introduce you to our producer, Flavia Baker?"

Saul barely recognized the woman who had played Katisha so well and was introduced. He shook hands and said, "I must congratulate you on such a wonderful production and on your part in it. Thank you."

As he shook hands, he felt a mild shiver of disgust as they touched, and she smiled at him and said, "You are Geoff's boss and Julia's I believe. Thanks, for letting them have the time off or change their duties or whatever, to rehearse and perform. Tell me, do you sing?"

Saul smiled and said, "No, I am afraid not, my wife here informs me I am tone deaf and have the singing voice of a corncrake!"

Anna said, "Believe me he is quite right but we have daughter with a good voice, she is studying music at school."

"Then she must come and join our junior section. They are putting on *Oliver* next spring."

Having been introduced to several other players Saul then politely excused himself, and they went out to the car park. Susan said, "It was actually not that bad, but a bit gruesome. That Katisha woman gave me the creeps though, but I rather liked the three school girls. Not my cup of tea but I know Mum and Sharon liked it. Please don't ask me to join!"

Anna said, "It is not compulsory; anyway, you have enough activities with your judo and your athletics and your swimming. It will be good for Sharon to have something she is good at instead of trying to keep up with you all the time. Right we must get home now because it is way past your bedtimes and we have a busy day tomorrow, and I have to make up the spare room."

"Why, who is coming, not Auntie Ruth?"

"No, we will tell you about it in the morning, now it is home to bed!"

Chapter Two

Saul was up early even though he was having a day off. He was quietly relaxing with a cup of coffee and reading the newspaper when the girls came down to the dining room. Anna joined them and over breakfast they discussed the plans for the day.

Susan asked, "Who is coming to stay, Dad, Mum, not Aunty Ruth again, please?"

Saul sighed and said, "No, not Ruth. It is my brother, Jake. He's coming for a few days."

The squeals of delight were shrill and long.

Susan said "Great, it is such fun when he comes. For a moment I thought you were going to say your other brother, but if it is Jake, he is so wicked."

"Yes, but you must try to behave yourselves, don't encourage him, your father has enough to cope with already. Please don't break the furniture again. It was bad enough last time. What was the damage then, Saul?"

"I think it was two chairs, one coffee table and three sheets; oh yes, and the garden bench. There is really no need for you to jump on him, you are getting too big now."

"But, Dad," said Sharon. "He loves it and you know it. He loves kids. Why isn't he married? Come to think of it, does he have any kids?"

"I suggest you ask him that, I am not my brother's keeper you know. Now chores first and then I think your mum wants to go shopping. Do you two want to come?"

During the shopping trip the conversation from the girls was almost exclusively about Jake's arrival. The only interruption to this was when they passed the music section of the shop and Anna had to refuse to buy more than one CD for each of them. Once home again Susan went off for swimming practice and Sharon admitted she had some homework to do. Saul perked up at this and wondered what had prompted such an unusual admission. He thoughtfully watched his younger daughter skip happily upstairs. He needed to write some letters and then loaded the dishwasher and sorted through some laundry before his wife got back with Susan. Anna and he unpacked the shopping and put it away.

Saul paused and said, "The girls are unusually quiet. What are they up to?"

Anna replied, "I have no idea, homework I expect. I told them they had to have it done before Jake arrives. What shall I cook for tonight?"

"I have a better idea, why don't we have a take away? I know the girls like it and so does Jake and it will save a lot of time."

"Saul, darling, is there any special reason Jake is coming to stay? Nothing is wrong in the family, is it?"

"Not that I know of, but it has been a while and I thought he might enjoy it, and I am sure the girls will. Right, I am going to walk the dogs, so I can be here when he arrives. Hector, Lysander, walkies. Then I must pop into the office for an hour or so; my new deputy is going to meet me there and I need to welcome him and see he has all he needs. I won't be that long."

As Saul got to his office, he saw Detective Inspector Withers waiting at the desk in the general office, reading the book of standing orders that had be to be kept in any department.

Saul went over and said, "I think you must be Alan Withers? Welcome to the Serious Crime Squad, come through to my office and we can have a chat."

Saul led the way and ushered Alan Withers into a seat.

"Have you moved into your quarters yet? Good, now tell me a bit about yourself, not the official stuff but about you as a person. If we are to work together, I need to know a bit about the real you. I believe you are a transferee?"

"Yes, sir, I am. I have moved into a flat in the centre of town and it will take me a day or two to get really straight, but I am available if it is urgent. What do you need to know?"

Saul instantly realized that Alan was either very nervous or rather shy or both. He said, "I think the best thing to do is to issue you with all the necessary things first, and then I can show you round, and you can get your office as you like it. Here is a car park pass and you will find the numbered plot in the yard outside and here is your personal radio and a mobile phone to use for work. I have got one of the lads to put in all the numbers I think you might need. Here is the list of codes, access codes and such that I suggest you learn. Now, do you have any special dietary requirements, or any religious requirements? I only ask because if and when we have to be away, I need to plan for them."

"Nothing special no, I don't eat a lot of meat and I take it I cannot use this phone other than for work?"

"That is up to you. Look I think you should get settled in for a few days but be available if we get called out to a major incident."

They chatted for about fifteen minutes and then Saul showed him round the squad room and then took him up to the canteen. He found conversation rather hard going with Alan and that he was rather reserved. It was obviously going to take time and tact to get to know the lad.

Saul pulled up on his drive only minutes before a rather dirty Land Rover pulled up beside him and his brother Jake got out accompanied by a huge mastiff like dog who instantly rushed over to Saul and putting its front paws on Saul's shoulders lovingly licked his face.

"Hercules, get down, yes, you are a very fine dog and I like you, but I do *not* need a wash. Hi, Jake, I see you still have this monster. Come on in, the girls are longing to see you. I have a good bottle of wine for later."

"Just one? I actually brought some to share anyway."

Jake was a very large man, slightly taller and much wider than Saul with a huge mop of rather long red hair and a huge red beard. He was dressed in casual countryside clothes and had big work boots on.

He approached Saul and gave him a massive bear hug and said, "Are you all right, bro? Long time no see! Come on, I am longing to meet the girls again. I take it the boys are away?"

"Saul said, "Yes, one at uni, and the other at work on the Isle of Man. Anna has made up your room and the girls are very excited. No, lad, don't bother taking your boots off. Come on in and we'll get your stuff in later."

As they got to the hallway there were excited yelps from the two girls who came running down the stairs two at a time or more and hurtled themselves at Jake, who give them big hugs and said, "Come on, you two, I have presents in the car for both of you. Help me unload."

Once everything was inside and the three dogs had had a play in the garden and Hercules had drunk all the contents of the dog's water bowl, Anna handed out mugs of tea and they went into the lounge and sat down. Then the dogs tried to sit on top of them and had to be turfed off to lie on the dog beds in the room.

The afternoon went very well and there was much laughter. Saul consulted with Anna what he should get for the takeaway. They were talking quietly in the kitchen, and Saul said, "Sorry, love, but I asked my new deputy, Alan Withers, if he would like to join us this evening. He has just moved into his flat from down south somewhere and knows no one and I need to get to know him. I think that is going to be a bit difficult. He is shy and rather standoffish. Could you try to work some of your magic on him, make him relax?"

"Really, Saul, you are impossible! Yes, all right but please tell me he isn't another one like Celia your last deputy. I know you found working with her very difficult sometimes. Yes, you became friends in the end, but she resented you."

"Yes, I know. I actually find this lad, well chap, because he is at least thirty, rather difficult to read. Standoffish, and a little arrogant but I may be wrong. I just want him to relax with me that's all."

"Well, if he is introduced to your brother, he won't be standoffish for long. Saul, when is Jake going to grow up? He told me he needs your advice about something, but wasn't very specific, something to do with land?"

"Land, I wonder if he is finally going to settle down? I know he was thinking of going into farming, but he knows precious little about it, back here in the UK anyway. He has been abroad for many years. I know he isn't short of a bob, he got lucky with some sort of mining I think it was, no doubt he will explain in his own good time."

Alan Withers arrived a few minutes later and was introduced and then the meal was delivered. Anna soon got chatting to him while Jake and Saul discussed the family problems with each other. The two girls asked many questions about Saul's other brother and Jake began to tell them a few tales of when he had grown up with Saul as his elder brother. Saul slipped out to the garden and then a nearby park with the three dogs before returning with them and finding Alan much more at ease, and then Alan took his leave as he needed to make up his bed before getting to sleep. The two girls sniggered slightly at this and after Alan had left, Saul looked at them and said suspiciously, "What are you two up to?"

Their reply of, "Nothing, Dad," did not make him feel any easier. The girls were duly sent off to bed. Saul watched them giggling together as they headed upstairs. He popped up to say goodnight a bit later and was astonished to find them already apparently asleep.

Once downstairs Anna wanted to relax in the lounge with a film, so Saul and Jake adjourned to Saul's study where Saul offered him a whisky.

"No thanks, brother, I would rather have some more of this superb wine if there is any."

Saul laughed and said, "Well we had better get another bottle from the lounge then."

"Yes, and I brought some, I'll fetch it and we can settle it down." In the lounge Jake looked at several of the bottles in the wine rack and said, "Saul, whoever brought you these wines not only spent a fortune but knew a lot about fine wines."

"Yes, she did. They were left to us, together with these beautiful crystal goblets. She was a special friend."

"A woman? These beautiful goblets are depicting Diana. I knew a Diana; she was the only woman I could ever have married. If you must know, I'm still in love with her. We worked together for a while, abroad, not that long ago. Never mind, what we were doing."

"I don't suppose she was an orchid expert, or had a special way with dogs?"

"Never saw her with dogs. It was in the Far East"

"Come with me to the study, Jake. Were you by any chance working for the government?"

"We might have been, but it wasn't under my name. She was called Diana Brown, and she was a remarkable woman. Someone got bitten by a snake, and she saved his life. For the first and only time I fell deeply in love, which at my age means forever, if the wise women are to be believed. I never saw her again. I couldn't stay out there, not after the job was over, not without her. I came home to try and forget her, but I can't. It serves me right, in a way. I've broken a few hearts in my time, now I'm being paid back in spades."

Saul pointed out a photograph on the desk top in the study, and Jake looked at it. He picked it up and gazed at it. "Yes, that's her. I don't suppose you'd give me this?"

"No, I won't. She meant a lot to me and Anna too. We knew her as Diana Green, but were told she had died. Knowing what she did, that means I know what you were doing. Let's leave it at that, shall we?"

"Can I get a copy made? I find the only woman I have ever really loved, and you tell me she's dead?"

Saul was startled to see tears in his brother's eyes. He put his hand on Jake's arm, and said, "The last time I saw you cry, Jake, was when you were nine, and our dog died. You care that much for this woman?"

"Yes, if you must know. I'll doubt I will ever get over it, even in time. She was brilliant, could out fox me, out argue me, was brave, she could even beat me at chess. She could cook better than me, and yet she hid most of her talents, but I got a glimpse of a goddess, just occasionally, when she chose to let her guard down. She was the most secretive woman I ever met. I know only what she let me see. I've a good brain, but she was way above my league. You know she saw everything, far more than I did, but she understood what she saw, where I couldn't always."

"I said Diana Green was dead, Jake. You are coming to us over Christmas? I think you should. We may have another house guest, then. Her name will probably be Black, or White, or Pink, but you might find her rather interesting. Just keep all this to yourself."

"Oh, I see, well I think I do. There is still hope? I can't wait. Oh, don't worry, I won't tell anyone. I never have yet. Believe it, I'll be here. Wild horses wouldn't stop me. Thanks, Senior, I owe you, and if you ever tell anyone you saw me cry, I'll skin you alive!"

"You haven't called me that in a few years, it is good we can catch up on a few things."

The rest of the evening was spent in happy relaxation.

The next morning Saul and Anna were woken to an outraged bellow from Jake's room and went in to find the girls had almost tied him in the bed. The girls were giggling helplessly with mirth and Jake was threatening to get them.

"It isn't so bad, but last night you little buggers had made an apple pie bed and when I got into it, I am afraid I put a foot through the sheet. I am sorry, Anna, I will replace it. I suppose it pays me back for all the pranks I have played on you girls. They have character, Saul, I am beginning to rather like your family!"

Saul smiled and said, "No, Jake, I am sure we can manage to replace one sheet. I doubt it was a new one, Anna knows better than that. Now I know why you girls were being so good yesterday, now untie him, and get down to breakfast."

The whole family went to a huge wildlife park where they all had a great time and Jake was a fountain of information about some of the animals and told stories of his times in the African bush where he had lived for some years.

Once back at the house they took the dogs for a walk and were just settling down to a good supper when the phone went. Saul picked up the phone on the desk. "Catchpole. Yes, where? Yes, I'll come straight away. Tell him I'm on my way and get Alan Withers to meet me there. I know where it is, I was I was there two nights ago. Have Scenes of Crime been called?"

Saul picked up his briefcase and car keys, and said, "I'm sorry, Jake, work calls. This one isn't too far, I've no idea when I'll be back. Will you be all right?"

"Go play, Inspector Morse, then."

"I see myself more as an extended Jack Frost."

Saul arrived at the theatre to be met by the duty inspector, who he had known for some years. "OK, John, tell me the score."

"Right, they were putting on The Mikado. There was some sort of mock execution during some song. It's not my thing, but there was this axe, a big show one. This man picked up this axe, and he says it sort of collapsed when he raised it and went down on this other man's neck and it took his head off. It was razor sharp. There was a doctor in the audience, and he declared the man dead immediately. We've touched nothing, and already have details of everyone in the audience, and the cast are backstage."

"Was the show being videoed?"

"I'll find out."

"Please. Who had the axe?"

"A character called Pooh Bear?"

"Pooh-Bar, not Geoff Bickerstaff?"

"Yes, that's right. He's in deep shock, the doctor is with him now. Says he's almost catatonic."

"He is also a member of my team, a DS. Get me that video, and are the cast being watched?"

"Yes, sir."

"As soon as DI Withers gets here, send him through to me. I'd better have a look. Can you find me a few programmes?"

Hardened as he was to sudden death, Saul felt sick. The axe was lying by the body and the blade was smeared faintly with blood. The heat of the lights was almost overpowering and there were several smells: salt, urine and vomit amongst them. He stared at the body which had a dribble of blood from the severed neck and then he saw the head some feet away lying on the stage. It had a trickle of blood escaping from the mouth and nose. He began to retch, so he left quickly, and got control of himself in the cooler air on the stairs backstage, although it did not smell any better. He was not the only person to feel sick.

He walked back into the auditorium and saw the stunned expressions of the orchestra, who were sitting either in the orchestra pit or in the stalls. The conductor was sitting slumped in the front row. Saul decided that to sit down was a very good idea and sank into the seat beside him.

"Did you see what happened?"

"Yes, I did, I wish I hadn't. Thank God they have drawn the curtains. It was ghastly, I couldn't believe it at first, thought it was some kind of joke. As soon as I realized I stopped the music. The stage manager lowered the curtain real quick. Poor, poor Cyril, and poor Geoff. He dropped the axe and sank down and put his hand out, but there was nothing he could do, no pulse to find, just blood pumping out. Who are you, anyway?"

"The detective in charge. As soon as the audience have all gone, I want you and the orchestra to make your way out of the foyer, where you can tell my officers your details, and what you all saw and heard."

"Thanks, most of them didn't see it, but a few did. The horn player threw up, and the percussionist. The second oboe fainted, along with several of the audience. Do you think we could get a drink, or even a cup of tea?"

"Of course you can, I think you all might need one."

"I think so, if not, I'll make sure they can."

Saul looked up as Alan Withers walked over to him and got up and walked towards the stage apron. "Alan, I trust your stomach is strong, get a goon suit on, and come with me. Ah, Inspector, did you find the video?"

"I did, sir, I have it here."

"Please will you get it straight to photographic, get it copied, and a statement from the person who was videoing the show? I also need copies of any photographs taken, of this or any of the other shows. Alan, it's not nice, but you need to see this."

Saul felt rather guilty when he was just a little gratified that Alan was very sick. A little of the confidence went, together with the contents of Alan's stomach.

"Are you all right, son?"

"No, sir, I'm not. I've seen a few, but not like that. It's so clinical, so vicious, so brutal and so final. It's macabre, rather Edgar Alan Poe."

"Yes, it is. We need to wait until forensics have finished, then I want to see that axe. Colin, have we found the prop one yet?"

The Scenes of Crime officer nearby looked up and said, "Not yet, guvnor. We are trying to get this tied up. We can move the body and the head now. Shall we?"

"The sooner the better, keep looking, we need to find it. Alan, are you up to seeing the cast?"

"Yes, sir, I'm sorry, I don't make a habit of throwing up, I promise. I'm better now."

The scene in the Green Room was one of total shock and depression. The men were sitting silently. Geoff Bickerstaff was silent and unmoving in a corner, with a man Saul assumed was the doctor, and with a paramedic beside them. Saul went over, crouched down, and said, "Geoff, it's Saul Catchpole."

Geoff looked up and began trembling. "Sir, I didn't know, please help me, this is a nightmare."

"It's all right, Geoff. You know we will look after you. I want you to go with this lady here, please? Who is the person in charge here, a manager or someone?"

Saul looked round and one lady said, "Jeanette is in the props room. The stage manager, Simon Hobbs is still in the wings with one of your officers."

"Thank you, Jane Waters, I think Peep-Bo?"

"That's me. I work at the local pharmacists. I live just down the road from here. I'll show you down to the props room."

"If you would. Where should the axe be kept when it's not on stage?"

"It should be here. I was telling your officer, it went missing for two days last week, from here, just before the pre-final rehearsal. It came back just before the dress rehearsal. We had to use a quick mock up. Is Geoff all right? I was horrified at what happened. I put the real axe, which is made of papier mâché on stage last night, in its normal place. I checked it before curtain up this evening, so did Geoff, he's very thorough. I even picked it up and made sure it was all right. Geoff and I said how murderous it looked, and then he went back to the dressing room, just before the overture."

"Who could have replaced it with the other one?"

"Anyone, the whole chorus, and most of the cast. The stage is full, with people getting on and off, the wings are chaos, a lot of the time. The costumes are big and bulky, with huge sleeves, as you saw; anyone could hide almost anything."

"Did you see what happened?"

"Oh yes, I did. I was off stage, in the wings. I saw Geoff pick up the axe. Ko-Ko picked up the chopping block, he sits briefly on it, before the trio. Geoff only had a very short time to get the axe. He turns, dances round on 'I must decline' then Pish-Tush kneels down, Geoff picks up the axe, raises it, and brings it down in a swing. Pish-Tush springs up, and Geoff was supposed to drop the axe, by the block, and him and Pish-Tush bring them off after the song and give them to me, and I put them down and bring them down after act one."

"From what I can remember, it was very ornate?"

'Yes, Flavia insisted on putting it in, I made it specifically. She wanted it to be very flashy, she likes to make things flashy. I saw Geoff look very surprised when he picked it up, like it was much heavier than he expected. Once it had happened, I went on stage, and although I didn't touch the false one, I did look at it. Have you seen it? There has been a lot of bad feeling because of what I can best describe as partner swapping. Cyril's wife has been playing away but Cyril found out about it. He's The Mikado, everybody knew about it. I'm afraid it happens sometimes. The Mikado's wife had been seeing Nanki-Poo, whose wife isn't in the cast, she's helping with the make-up. Last week, Monday I think it was, there was a huge row in the Green Room. I wasn't there, but I know that Geoff stopped it and told everyone to behave themselves. For a quiet man he can be quite authoritative sometimes. He's one of your lot, I believe, nice man. Is he all right?"

"No, he isn't. Who locks up? Who has keys?"

"I have a set, the stage manager, Simon Hobbs, Flavia, and one of the stage hands."

Saul said, "Please will you show me around? I mean everywhere, where all the doors are, what keys open what and where all the passages go and where things are stored."

Twenty minutes later he was back where they had started.

"From what I saw the axe was very cleverly constructed to hinge. Is anything else missing or different?"

"Yes, the block. Ko-Ko lifted it and said it looked quite heavy too. I haven't touched it but it's not the one I put there. I found the real one, on the stairs as I came down. I brought it in here. This one is very light; it's just a stool, with a bit of plywood on it."

Saul looked at the stool she pointed out, and said, "I see, from what you and Sandra were saying, something has been going on?"

"What do you want me to do, how can I help? I know better than to touch anything. I watch *Midsummer Murders* and *Frost!*"

"Could I borrow your keys and then I'll get someone to run you home. Do you live alone? I can get someone to stay with you. I can tell how upset you are."

"Thank you, but I have elderly parents at home. I'm a widow. I'll get a taxi if it's easier."

"I would like a statement. Will it upset your parents if the officer takes a statement from you at your home?"

"I doubt it. They will be asleep by now. This was murder, wasn't it? It has to be."

"It looks like it, yes. If you feel nervous or afraid, I will happily get you a guard."

"No, dear, how kind, it is not for me that I am afraid. I doubt I am in any danger. I make a point of not upsetting anyone or getting involved in the petty squabbles that happen. You are kind, I can tell. I must say, you are not quite what I expected, somehow."

"Oh dear, what did you expect?"

"I don't know, someone bombastic, loud, bossy, I suppose. From what our officers were saying I rather expected God to walk in. They hold you in great respect, you know, and not a little admiration."

"The respect is quite mutual, I am lucky enough to have a hard working, capable team, very professional. You don't miss much, do you?"

"I do a lot of people watching. You care, I think, are you artistic?"

"I paint, when I have time. Ah, Paul, have you news?"

"Yes, sir, they have found the real axe, hidden under a bench in the male dressing room, behind a rack of costumes for the second act. It's been bagged. What do you want me to do?"

"Please take Mrs Cadogan home and take a statement from her, you know what I want. This sergeant will take you home, madam, and I promise he won't wake your parents."

"I'd be delighted to. Incidentally the whole cast will be here at noon tomorrow. The whole team is here now, and SOCO has almost finished on stage. Mrs Cadogan, please, come with me."

Jeannette handed her keys to Saul and he gave her his card, and he locked the room as they left together. He went up to the main stage, and found the stage manager. Simon Hobbs was a chubby, balding little man with a bright ginger goatee beard, and was acting very camp. He saw Saul and minced towards him.

"Oh dear, oh dear, oh dear. This is just frightful. Just simply too ghastly. I doubt my nerves will ever recover!

I'm very sensitive you know, like a delicate bloom. I'm almost wilting now, that this should happen on my stage! It's all about jealously you know. The goings on! You have no idea, I thought show business was bad enough, but all these aspiring talents! I was an actor you know, but I went into stage management. Now, sweetie, how can I help you?"

Saul sighed. He could do without a lovey. He asked for, and was given a copy of the stage directions, and then, collecting Simon's keys, sent him home. He called over one of his women officers. "Caroline, please take Mr Hobbs home, and get a full statement from him."

"Oh no, dearie, my partner Charlie will be wildly jealous if I bring a woman home. Can't it be that dishy young policeman over there? I do like a man in uniform, you know. Charlie does too."

"Mr Hobbs, behave yourself! I need that officer here. WDC Connors has the experience to take a proper statement from you, as such a vital witness. If Charlie doesn't like it, he can complain to me. Don't make things more difficult for me, please?"

Simon Hobbs gave a pathetic simpering giggle and went to fetch his coat. Caroline looked reproachfully at Saul. "Thanks, guv, I really needed that!"

"I'm sorry, I'll buy you a drink, no several, for it. If I send that young PC, I doubt he'd get out unmolested.

Hobbs knows something, I'm sure of it. This outrageous flirting is hiding something. Ring me if you need help."

"Yes, sir, but you owe me big time!"

"I know. I'd go myself, but I'm not sure even I'd be safe. I want him onside, not angry at being rejected. Please?"

"I see, OK. Incidentally, the hospital rang, they have sedated Geoff, he's going to be sleeping for a while. I went and got his wife, and took her there. She'll ring if she needs us. Where will you be?"

"On the mobile. We meet at the office at nine, if you can."

Saul waited until the cast and the orchestra had left the theatre. Once the stage lights were off, and the police officers had gathered in the auditorium, he said, "Are we finished with forensics? Good, how about photographs? Well done, I want someone here, front and back all night. The rest of you go home, get some rest, as it's now way past midnight. If anything happens here, ring me straight away. Inspector, can you get the building covered? Thank you. I doubt it will be very long before the press gets hold of this, and I don't want them coming in here."

"I think press office have already had a call. The caretaker is here, sir. He wants to know what it is you want him to do. Seems a nice chap, ex Para; he thinks he might have some information for us."

"Thank you, Derek, please see what he knows, and get him to check round with you, before we lock up, to see if anything is out of place. I'm going to see Geoff, and I'll meet you all either here or at HQ in the morning. I'll also watch this copy of the video."

Saul had a headache by the time he left, and he got to the hospital, where he was taken to see Geoff, and found him deeply asleep. He sat down by the bed and looked at the heavy set, gentle man who had worked with him for some years. Geoff was a pillar of strength on the squad: he was gentle, able, reliable, and very clever. Saul wondered if he was allowing his personal admiration and liking for the man to cloud his judgement. He had not been sitting by the bed very long when Geoff's wife, Theresa, came into the room.

"It's all right, Theresa, I won't wake him. I'm so sorry, what can I do to help?"

"Thanks for coming, I don't know how to help him either. He kept saying he didn't know, and he wasn't a murderer. You don't think he is, do you?"

"No, I don't, of course I don't. To be fair to him, I must investigate it correctly, but I do not suspect him. Have you anyone who can be with you? I'll stay if you want me to?"

"Thank you, but our son is coming; he's driving up from Reading, and he should be here soon. This could destroy Geoff, you know. He's already racked with guilt; he's such a gentle man, he'd never hurt anything, he can't even kill a spider!"

"Yes, I know that. I do need to tell you that whatever help either of you need, is yours, just ask me. If I can help, ring me, anytime. Here is my home number as well as my works one. He's not only one of my best officers, he's a friend. I'll stay until your son gets here, if you would like?"

"You must have lots of things to do, I can't ask that of you."

"You haven't, I offered, because I want to. Shall we get a cup of coffee? The nurse said he won't wake, and if he does, they'll call us. Come on, I could do with one, even if you couldn't."

Over a cup of coffee in an almost deserted hospital canteen, Theresa broke down and cried, and Saul offered her a clean handkerchief, and listened. When she had calmed down, and was sniffling into the handkerchief, she looked up at him, and saw the gentle expression in Saul's face. He smiled at her, and said, "I promise you, Theresa, I will find out who did this, and they will be brought to justice. I know Geoff was set up for this, and I will grant no mercy to this killer, whoever it is."

"Yes, I know you will. Geoff says you always get your man. Please prove it wasn't him. Oh, that's my son, thank goodness he's here."

Saul couldn't have mistaken the tall young man for anyone else, he was so like Geoff. He hugged his mother and then said, "Who are you?"

"I'm Geoff's boss. If I can do anything to help I will. Theresa, do you want me to stay?"

"Thanks, sir, but I'll be all right now Jo is here. I know you had a lot else to do, but you made time for me and him, and for listening. You'd better have your hanky back."

"Keep it, I have a plentiful supply. Promise me, you will ring if I can help?"

"I will."

Saul made it home not long before dawn, crept into the house, and headed to bed, having noticed there was a small table in pieces in the hall, obviously awaiting repair.

Chapter Three

By the time the team assembled at nine the next morning, Saul had watched the video, and was going through the statements already obtained. He noted that the premises of some of the cast had been searched. He had just finished speaking to the coroner and then rang the hospital and the force welfare officer. He handed out some papers to the squad. Attached to each was a programme of the show. He ran through it with them.

THE MIKADO
OR
THE TOWN OF TITIPU
BY
SIR WILLIAM SCHWENCK GILBERT
AND
MUSIC BY
SIR ARTHUR SULLIVAN

CAST

THE MIKADO OF JAPAN	TOM CANTONE
NANKI-POOH	JOHN KIPPS
KO-KO	RICHARD DEARKIN
POO-BAH	GEOFFREY BICKERSTAFF
PISH-TUSH	CYRIL JONES
GO-TO	DAVID BAKER
KATISHA	FLAVIA ALICIA BAKER
YUM-YUM	SONYA WOOD-SMYTHE
PETTI-SING	JULIA PELLOW
PEEP-BO	JANE WATERS

CHORUS OF SCHOOLGIRLS, NOBLES, GUARDS AND COOLIES

THERESA BICKERSTAFF	ALOYSIUS BAKER
SYLVIA CANTONE	ALEXIS BISHARA
SANDRA COLLINGWOOD	STEVEN DALE
SARA DEARKIN	SOLOMON EBDEN
NATASHA HOKUDU	PTOLEMY EMMETT
ANITA JONES	MAURICE FABRE
SOPHIA KAUR	STEPHEN JONES

41

ZAPHIR KAUR	ANDREW PERKINS
BRIDGET O'SHEA	PAUL O'SHEA
SARAH PEACOCK	AMJIT SINGH
JUNE SMITHERS	TAJUPAH SINGH
MARY SUMMERTON	COLIN WATERS
JANET WATERS	AARON WHITE
SUSAN WILSON	MICHAEL WOOD-SMYTHE
SYBIL WITHERSPOON	CHARLOTTE ZACHMRMUS

PRODUCER

FLAVIA ALICIA BAKER

MUSICAL DIRECTOR

HAYDEN DAVIES

STAGE MANAGER

SIMON HOBBS

WARDROBE/PROPS

JEANETTE CADOGAN

While everyone read through the programme, Saul said, "Alan will allocate your actions, but most of the cast and stage hands are at the theatre at noon. Before we go any further I need to explain something. All of us, except Alan Withers here, know and have worked with Geoff Bickerstaff. The best way we can help him is to do this enquiry properly. I need to know how all of you feel about this. At this time, I cannot eliminate him as a suspect, and I don't think he would want me to. I do not believe he knew what would happen, and I am sure he is innocent, but I need to prove it. If anyone suspects anything, or out of friendship or misguided loyalty are reluctant to say what you know, don't be. Tell me or DI Withers, however unimportant you may think it is. We owe it to Geoff, Julia, and ourselves, not to mention the victim, to be totally unprejudiced about this, and do the best job we can."

"Sir. I for one believe him to be innocent. I know I may also be a suspect just the same as everyone there. I can tell you that Geoff and his wife kept out of the wrangling, as I did. He did tell them to leave the affairs of the heart outside the theatre, last week.

"Most of the cast, and those who didn't were soon told all about it. I'm not really sure who is carrying on with who. I've only been in the society a few months, and although I'll stop for a drink, I'm not in the 'set'."

"Thanks, Julia, I think I'm about to find out. A Sandra Collingwood is coming to see me, do you know her?"

"Yes, nice woman, one of the stalwarts, she's on the committee, I would best describe her as dedicated, hardworking and a bit strait-laced. She and Jeanette Cadogan are friend; they always come together. I'm not sure about those two. The gossips say they are more than friends, but they say a lot of things that are not true."

Sandra and Jeanette came in together to see Saul, and over a coffee in an interview room, Sandra said, "Thank you for seeing us. This year's production has been fraught with problems. There has always been the odd affair, but last year was worse than normal. This year Tom and Anita have been so indiscreet. Cyril must have seen what was going on, it was his third marriage you know. He fell heavily for Anita three years back. He must have known what she was like, because she was married to someone else in the cast then. Cyril made sure she wasn't going to make money out of him. He was a very rich man, you know, his building firm is very large and successful."

"So I understand. Who was Anita married to then?"

"Ptolemy Emmett, he was gutted, poor man, at the time, he's only just come back to the society this year. He has a superb voice. It's obvious to me, and others I think, that he's still in love with Anita. When it became apparent that she was willing to stray from Cyril, I'm sure he was hoping to get her back. He and Tom fell out. Tom can be very scathing, and he's very arrogant, that's why he makes such a good Mikado."

"I see. Tell me, who is romantically involved with whom, in the society?"

Jeanette laughed, and said, "How tactfully you put that. You want to know if Sandra and I are an item, if we are lesbian lovers. No, we are not, we have been friends for years. Oh, I know what the gossip says, if you don't fall for a man, then you are obviously gay. Sandra and I were at school together. All right, Ko-Ko, that's Richard, his marriage went through a rocky patch last year; his wife was having an affair, and not for the first time. They only stick together for the sake of the children, he's a nice chap. Anita and Tom are having a very public affair, and Sylvia has been seeing John Kipps, that's Nanki-Poo. His wife Lizzie doesn't seem to care at all, she's not in the cast. There are some moralistic members of the society, Sonja and Michael Wood-Smythe, they have not long been married, and the Singh family, of course, who are a bit shocked by some of what is going on, but rise above it. They are so keen to become English, they embrace the society. The father, Amjit, has a wonderful sense of humour. We are very lucky we have several ethnic minorities. Ptolemy's mother was Egyptian, the Singhs, Natasha Hikodu is Japanese, studying at the university, and she's been a great help with this production."

"What is she studying?"

"Chemistry, I think. Then there is Alex Bishara, such a talented musician, he is from Cyprus. If you really want the gossip, Simon Hobbs has been flirting outrageously with Maurice Fabre, who is not that way inclined, and may be chasing Bridgett O'Shea."

"Now these two, they have both been members since they joined as juniors, and no, I have no idea if or who she's involved with."

"Thank you. Was there something else you wanted to tell me?"

The two women looked at each other, and after a pause, Jeanette said, "Yes there is, we think you should know something that happened last year. We talked it over earlier, and while we were a bit perplexed when it happened, now it seems it might have more serious connotations. While we were rehearsing for *Iolanthe*, something rather odd happened. Tom was playing Private Willis, and there was a dreadful row about casting with Flavia, Cyril and David, Flavia's husband, and some of the others. Geoff was Tom's understudy, and David wanted it. David rather likes to be the dependable 'I can step in and do anything in a crisis' person. Just after that we all went to a barbeque at Tom's house, except Geoff, who was working. I think that was before Julia joined. Some of the guests had the most dreadful stomach upsets afterwards, food poisoning, or something like that. Strangely, all the ones who got ill were the ones Tom had fallen out with. Someone said the prawns must have been tainted, but that's not so, because I ate them and I was fine. The only thing I didn't have was the wine, because I was driving."

"You think there was something in the wine?"

"I'm afraid I do."

"So do I. Jeanette is right. I was talking about it not long after to Natasha Hokudu; we sing in the sopranos together. She said it was almost as if they were suffering from the symptoms of mild arsenic poisoning."

"Did she?"

"Look, Mr Catchpole, Tom is a very able man, but he has a rather nasty streak. He was playing the Captain in *HMS Pinafore* a few years ago. He was so good as the sadistic autocratic man that I thought it wasn't all acting.

"Do you remember that incident, what, four or five years ago, when he got accused of harassment at his school? It was a young male student teacher, and it all got hushed up, but it sounded rather odd?"

"I'd forgotten that, Sandra. Yes, the young man had complained or something, and Tom made his life hell. Didn't it have something to do with the brakes on his car?"

"No, it was the brakes on his motorbike: they had been tampered with, but they couldn't prove it was Tom. I know the police were involved."

"You don't happen to remember this young man's name?"

"Kevin Thomas. I remember because they are names I know."

"I'll check it out. Who else might have wished Cyril harm?"

"Flavia doesn't like him much. Did you know, that isn't her real name?"

"No, what is it?"

"Frances Alice. She didn't think it sounded artistic enough. She lumbered that poor son of hers with Aloysius, he's gay, incidentally. He and Simon Hobbs had a fling not long ago."

"A serious one?"

"I'm not sure. I don't want to tell you to suck eggs, but I do think you should consider Tom."

"I will, please rest assured of that, what does he teach?"

"Physics and engineering, he's a head teacher now, but he is clever with his hands. Please don't tell him we told you, or we might have an accident ourselves. We thought you should know, but as you can see, we have no proof. It may just be the ramblings of two middle-aged women, but we are concerned."

"Ladies, you are not rambling, you are observant, and this is helping me a great deal. What can you tell me about Hobbs?"

"He came three years ago. He's very good at what he does, quite insufferable sometimes, but good for the society. He's paid, of course. He does run an efficient stage."

"Yes, he does, and he is very observant, he doesn't miss a trick, everything is planned to the last-minute detail."

"I see. Anything else?"

"Not really, but Flavia made such a thing about including the mock execution, not long before the final run of rehearsals. It was only a small bit, and could easily have been left out, but she insisted it was put in. I wondered why."

"Do you know, Mrs Cadogan?"

"No. For a small bit, it made a lot of extra work. I gave up protesting about Flavia's last-minute artistic touches a long time ago. It's easier to just do it!"

"I know the feeling! I know you have made a statement, Mrs Cadogan, have you, Mrs Collingwood?"

"Not yet, I'll do it at the theatre later, if I may."

"Thank you. Do either of you ladies need a lift anywhere?"

"No, we have my car, we are both going to the theatre after we've had a coffee. When will the funeral be?"

"Not yet, I'm afraid, there has to be an autopsy, and an inquest. The coroner will probably release the body as soon as he can."

"Yes, of course. I expect Flavia will insist we re-open, as a tribute to Cyril or something equally dramatic. For all her artistic temperament, she has no sensitivity at all."

When Saul arrived at the theatre about twelve thirty, he was pleased to see that his team of officers were well organized, with tables set up where they were taking statements.

Alan Withers saw him come in and came over to greet him. "Sir, most of the cast and company have come in. Mrs Baker is making a fuss saying she will only talk to the officer in charge, and only then in private. She bluntly told me I wouldn't do!"

"Oh, did she? I want to talk to her anyway, and I want you with me. This is well organized, Alan, I am impressed. Have you hit any problems?"

"Yes, and no, your team is very efficient, and know exactly what to do, but they seem rather reserved, even suspicious of me. Paul one of the skippers subtly suggested that I swap round a couple of the officers, and then asked me if I would take some advice from him. I said, yes I would."

"What was the advice?"

"He suggested I ask for volunteers for certain tasks, rather than just dishing them out. He explained the team have worked together a rather long time and each member knows what they are good at. He also said that none of them will let you down and they are a very hard-working lot, very conscientious."

"He's quite right, they are. Each has their own, quite individual strengths. There is no way you could know them yet. I'll tell you why they are wary of you, your predecessor put all their backs up wanting it done her way. She came around eventually and now I miss her input. What else did he say?"

"He just told me a bit about the team."

"Come on, Alan, he said more than that. You are going to be my right-hand man, so we need to be able to be totally frank with each other. I must be able to have your candid opinion, and no secrets between us. I will be straight with you and expect the same back."

"All right, yes he told me a bit about you, and how you work. How you seldom order, you make suggestions, and he said if I had an ounce of sense, to listen and follow them or discuss it with you before I didn't. He also told me not to make you lose your temper, but I already knew that!"

"Yes, I am reputed to have a fierce temper, the fact that I have never lost it with any of my team is quite irrelevant! Yes, I have a temper, but the reputation suits me very well. What else did he say?"

"He told me you had a DC on the squad for a short while, but he didn't last long because of his racist and sexist attitude. He told me this was a non-prejudicial working environment and anyone who steps out of line doesn't last long!"

"That is true as well. Did he tell you why?"

"No, he said I'd realize soon enough."

"I'll tell you. I'm Jewish and I've been subjected to racism, often enough to know how destructive and distressing it can be, and how it can hinder good police work. Is that a problem for you?"

"No, not at all. I'm actually rather relieved, I can relate to that. I just haven't had your guts to admit to what I am. I've hidden my beliefs and true interests, I thought the less anyone knew about me the easier it would make my life, cowardly, I know."

"Then maybe, you would like to tell me?"

"Yes, all right. I'm a committed Christian. I'm vegetarian. And while I am interested in cars, football and computers, I am also studying with the Open University for a degree."

"In what?"

"Theology. I made the mistake of telling my previous governor once, and they froze me out, thought I was odd, not one of the boozy crowd."

"I understand what you are saying, and I don't have a problem with anyone following their own way, so long as we can work together and understand each other. Do you drink?"

"Yes, in moderation, but I don't move in the circles where it is important."

"Then we'll get on very well. You interest me, under that veneer of authority and quiet command, I think there is a rather sensitive man. Am I right?"

"Yes, sir, you are, I've always been afraid of showing a soft under belly, but it is there."

"I don't advertise mine, but it is there, and when you work as closely with a team as I do, it will show. Do you read a lot? I know you have an excellent education?"

"Yes, it is one of my greatest pleasures. How did you work that out?"

"Your reference to Edgar Allan Poe. Look, we need to take Mrs Flavia down a peg or two, we can get to know each other later."

In a small office in the foyer of the theatre, they sat round a small desk. Flavia drew breath to speak and waited for the admiring attention of the two men.

Before she could start, Saul said, "Mrs Baker, you can cut the histrionics, and start helping me, rather than trying to hinder me. Shall we start with your full name?"

She gave him a look of pure poison, and in an outraged voice said, "Flavia Alicia Baker. There is no need to be rude, I'm only talking to you because the chief constable said you had his complete confidence, I can't think why. You must understand the artistic temperament. Are you a Thespian?"

"No. I once played Shylock in the Merchant of Venice at school, but I wasn't very good, and so nervous I decided it wasn't my thing."

"What about you, young man?"

"I was Joseph in the school nativity play twice, and then I was in a school production of *The Happy Prince,* by Wilde. I was the prince, and I hated it."

"No dedication, I can see that. Of course, you need talent to begin with, which neither of you have, and then total commitment. Is this really a murder, not an accident?"

"Yes, it is. Shall we try again with your real name this time?"

"I told you, Flavia Alicia Baker, nee Smith."

"Not Frances Alice Baker, nee Smith, born 12 November 1949 at Reading?"

The look she gave Saul could have soured milk at a thousand paces. She drew in breath, and was about to speak, and then went silent for some time. The men waited patiently.

"Yes, all right, I don't know how you found that out. I needed to change my name for something more interesting, for the sake of my art, you see. That was years ago. You can call yourself what you like, it's not against the law."

"True, but you have used your real name quite recently, have you not?"

"You obviously know, and it didn't take you long to do some checking up, did it? It was all a silly mistake. I never meant to take anything; it's my time of life, the change, you know."

"Four times in three years? Once in Sheffield, twice here in Leeds, and once in Wakefield. Two cautions and two convictions, all for shoplifting."

"Yes, well, I get forgetful. Please don't tell anyone. I need this job with the society as producer. My husband knows, obviously, but no one else does."

"You had to tell him, when the probation officer saw you. No, I won't tell anyone, but I think you'll find several people in the society do know, and for their own reasons are being discreet, as you say, the society needs your considerable talents. I came and saw the show earlier this week, and I was very impressed!"

The pompous woman had vanished, and a crestfallen pathetic creature sat in front of them. Gradually she began to relax. She looked up at Saul, and said, "You *do* understand, I may have misjudged you. Yes, I have made some dreadful mistakes, and I regret them. What do you want to know?"

They talked through the production, the casting and rehearsals. Flavia was very frank and rather blunt about some of the abilities of most of the cast. She was intelligent and observant. Alan said very little but watched as Saul coaxed more information out of her.

When Saul went outside to answer a telephone call she turned to Alan and said, "You haven't much to say for yourself."

"I don't need to. I'm learning from a master, he's a very clever chap. I'm just finding that out. I think you are very wise to confide in him."

"If I try to hide anything, he will see it, that I do know. Now I know why he's in charge. I would never have told anyone half of what I just told him. I see why the chief's so confident of him. I'm sure he was an excellent Shylock."

Saul came back into the room and said, "I'm sorry about that, I just had some important information. Why did you put this mock execution into the production at such a late stage?"

Flavia looked slightly embarrassed. She looked over at Alan and then back at Saul, and said, "I was asked to."

"Who by?"

"Tom Cantone. I didn't think it was necessary, but he sort of insisted on it. He said it would add something to the song."

"In what way did he insist?"

"I don't know how he found out, but he knew about the shoplifting. I wanted Geoff to be the Mikado, but when we were casting, it was then Tom told me he knew, and 'suggested' that he got the part. I didn't see any harm in the mock execution thing, so I made sure it was done well."

"You gave an accurate sketch of the axe to the props manager, Jeanette Cadogan. Who did that sketch?"

"Tom did, I think. He said he'd researched what it should look like, off the net, and it was very decorative, with that thick handle and complex head."

"Who else knows about this being Tom's idea?"

"Simon Hobbs. He challenged me about it, said it was a lot of work, and I told him Tom wanted it, even though Tom wasn't even in that scene."

"What else did Tom 'suggest'?"

"One or two things, some of them very good ideas, He insisted I played Katisha, when the others wanted to give it to Julia, who is very good. Tom said he was going to be the Mikado, and as such he had the right to say who played Katisha. Julia, thankfully, only wanted the part of Pitti-Sing, in which she is excellent."

"I thought so. Were you at a barbeque at Tom's house in the summer?"

"Where we all went down with food poisoning, yes, but I wasn't affected, even though I ate the same as David and my son who were both ill."

"How did you get on with Cyril Jones?"

"All right. He tended to be a little fussy, meticulous and always precise, and knew his part and performed it well."

"But you didn't like him much?"

"Not much. He was a whinger, and moaned about things, ad nauseum. If he felt someone had slighted him, he would tell the world, like he did over Tom and Anita. He played the cuckolded husband very well. Geoff, bless him, stopped a huge row in the Green Room. How is he, do you know?"

"He's in deep shock, still and under sedation. He thinks everyone will think he is a murderer."

"That's nonsense, he's a kind, gentle man. You don't think that, do you?"

"No, I don't but others will, and we have to eliminate him. DI Withers has recorded everything you have said, and we will prepare a statement from it, which I will ask you to read through, and if you are in agreement with it, sign. If anything does occur to you, will you ring me?"

"Yes, I know I've behaved badly. Please, don't let out about my convictions."

"We won't. Do you know why Tom Cantone isn't here today?"

"Yes, he said something about being needed at school today. I don't know why, it's half term, he's coming in later. I've been thinking about the show. I wondered if we could do a memorial show at a future time, for Cyril and Anita. Do you think it would be appropriate?"

"I think you must discuss that with the committee and Mrs Jones, but please let me know if you do."

Out in the main part of the theatre, things were running smoothly, and after a quick check round, Saul said, "Come on, Alan, let's get a bite to eat. There is an excellent cafe just down the road that does both kosher and vegetarian food. I need to update you, then we must find out what we have got so far and plan our next moves. The press office is dealing with all the enquiries."

Over lunch, Saul and Alan discussed the case, and later they joined in another team meeting, and Alan and Paul organized the next round of enquiries while Saul opened the inquest into Cyril's death. When he returned, they watched the video of the murder and looked through the statements already taken. He read and then re-read Tom Cantone's statement, and then that of Anita Jones, the murdered man's widow.

He said to Alan, "I am not happy with these. I think we need to interview these two. Especially him, he's lying through his teeth."

Saul made it home about eight that evening, to be greeted by Hercules, who had the mangled remains of Saul's walking stick in his mouth. Anna explained that Jake was staying on for a few days and was due in with the girls, who he had taken to the new Harry Potter film. Jake had promised to mend the growing pile of broken furniture in the conservatory. They had a pleasant evening and an early night.

Chapter Four

Saul was up early the next morning, had breakfast and headed into work. When he got in there were only a couple of the squad in the office including Caroline Connors who looked at him and said, "You look tired, guv, are you all right?"

"More importantly, are you? I am sorry I sent you off with that Hobbs chap, but I thought you might do much better than a male officer. What did you find out?"

"The statement is on your desk, sir. They really were the most insufferable couple and so full of their own importance it took a while to get anything out of Hobbs. To say I intensely dislike him might be a fair call."

"Yes, but you got a statement."

"It is on your desk, sir, but I think you might need to see our Mr Hobbs and his partner again and separately this time. I sort of got the feeling that all was not well between them despite the act Hobbs was putting on."

"Your intuition is usually spot on, but I am not going alone, and I won't ask you to come either. I think I need to go with our new DI. Thanks, Caroline, I knew I could rely on you."

Saul read through a pile of statements and when Alan came in, he said, "Don't take your coat off we're going out immediately."

They got down to the yard and Alan said, "Yours or mine, sir?"

Saul smiled and said, "Yours, and then you can claim the mileage. Here is the address and it isn't that far, oh you have a satnav, that might help a lot."

On the journey round the ring road, they discussed what had turned up in the statements. Alan had read many of them before going home the previous evening. They pulled up at a block of rather modern flats and found a parking space and rang the appropriate bell and Hobbs answered. They went up to his flat on the third floor and rang the bell and were let into a very over decorated flat by Hobbs. He simpered and said, "Oh, how lovely, dearies, two luscious men coming to see me. Go on through to the sitting room, but please don't sit on the Louis XIV chair. I don't think it will take the weight of either of you. You darling policemen are all so large. Can I offer you a cappuccino or a latte or something more elegant like a prosecco?"

"Thank you but we are fine. Now we are really here to find out what you know, saw, and discovered about the tragedy."

"Well of course you are, dearie, and I will tell you what I know. Oh, how sweet, you are taking notes, are you, duckie? Right, I used to be on the stage and now I am a professional producer, director for a couple of companies. I went to this one three years ago. I leave the music to the musical director and my job is to put on a slick, good production with what are essentially a load of amateurs, who need getting up to a decent standard. Only the larger companies can afford me, but we always make a profit, well we did until now. People go to see a show and to marvel at it and be transported to another world for a couple of hours. This show was going to be brilliant. The Mikado has so much scope, and I was sort of given a free rein with costumes and props.

"There has been a lot of bitching and squabbling during rehearsals this time, affairs, and the like, which has made things rather awkward sometimes. I had to crack the whip a bit. Geoff bless him did install a bit of order. I will tell you, Flavia is a first-class bitch and almost impossible to work with. It is always about her! She is as sensitive to others' feelings as a block of granite. Now the first couple of performances went great, and then on the dreadful day one or two things were a bit out of kilter, odd if you know what I mean."

"In what way exactly?"

"Well people were not where they should have been. I always insist that if there is no need for anyone to be in the wings then they wait either in their dressing room or the Green Room where they must wait for their call. It is all timed well and it works. Quite why Tom was hanging around so early I do not know. He never should be there until much later, in fact he doesn't even get to the theatre until we are well into the first act."

"What else did you notice?

"The handkerchief, it shouldn't have been there."

"Where was it?"

"On the stairs leading to the dressing rooms. It is a thing about The Mikado, the Japanese don't use them."

"Go on."

"Look there have been a lot of strange things happening and I was a complete pratt not connecting them. Now to be frank, I am very scared because I think there is something, another agenda, that is wrapped round the production. I might well be next."

"Why would you think that?"

"It was something Tom said, after we got the curtains closed. He whispered to me, and told me to be careful and not rock the boat. Then he said I shouldn't trust anyone, even those close to me. I was somewhat surprised because I had no reason to think he might be concerned with my welfare; in fact, I always got the impression he despised me."

"Why?"

"I don't think he likes my sexuality."

"Anything else?"

"Well, I have been thinking things through, and I hope I am wrong, but several odd 'accidents' have nearly happened to me, around the theatre. Too many now I have thought it through. I nearly cut myself quite badly on a prop sword, at least that is what I thought it was, that was laying across my manager's door a couple of days ago. When I checked it, it was a real sabre, razor sharp. No one seemed to know how it had got there. Then there was the funny coffee that I found on my desk. I took one sip and threw it away. I was violently sick afterwards. I have been getting hate mail, here at the flat too. I asked my partner Charlie what he knew about it and he said nothing, but I don't really trust anyone now. I was under the impression he didn't really know any of the cast or the society, but I happened to glance at his phone and saw a text from Tom Cantone to him, which said *all is ready. Let me know when your part is done*. I didn't mention I had seen it."

Saul glanced across at Alan and then said, "Have you upset anyone in the cast?"

"Probably most of them, but only by telling them to stop playing prima donna and do as they were directed. I may have offended one or two, especially their egos but that comes with the job. I certainly had nothing against either poor Geoff or that poor murdered man, Cyril. I must admit I didn't like either of them much, but

I had no reason to hate them. Now, dearie, I do need to tell you something, you may not know. Tom and Alexis didn't like Cyril at all and neither did many other people. I have only been with this company a couple of years but there are all sorts of intrigues going on. I tried to stay out of it, or even rise above most of it."

Alan asked, "Tell me, Mr Hobbs, what do you think happened the other night?"

"Yes I've been racking my brains about it. Whoever made that other blade, the murder weapon shall we call it, knew what they were doing, and it had to be someone in the cast or stage crew, or props because it looked identical to the proper one. The block was different too. Recently lots of things have gone missing for a few days and then turned up, and I blamed the props, but they denied it."

Saul said, "I think, Mr Hobbs, we need to get all this down in a statement. I am going to need both your expertise and knowledge to help me on this. Can we get that written down now?"

Hobbs paused and then said, "Of course we can, but I need to tell you I have no intention of hanging around long enough for anyone to murder me. I want to get out and to safety until all this has been resolved. I was going to go down to stay with relatives at a place called New Milton, near the New Forest. I will happily give you the address, but I want to go today. I know I have to give my statement to you and the only reason I didn't go before is because I knew you would want to talk to me and to go would make you think I was doing a bunk and therefore suspect me. I was going to order a taxi as soon as I had seen you and catch a train. I have already put things out to pack and I have left a note for Charlie explaining. I hope he will understand. Of course, I will give you my number there and will happily return if you need me."

"You really are frightened? Then if that is the case, we will happily try to protect you. My detective inspector will take your statement now and then, Alan, maybe you can drop him off at the station and see him safely onto the train? Then no one but us will know where and when you went. Do you want a police escort to your relatives at the other end?"

Saul fielded a rather blank stare from Alan and then Alan smiled, nodded and said, "Yes of course, I will happily help, but we must have your address and contact details, and would you mind if we just held onto your passport until it is resolved? We cannot discount any one from our suspect list until we have more facts."

"My darling, you are worried about me, thank you of course, that's why I didn't want to go before I had seen you. I'll go get my passport and I have got everything ready to pack, but maybe you should check through to make sure I am not disposing of any evidence. I would love a lift. I will ring one of you to confirm I got there, from the phone at the house if you like."

He left the room and Alan wrote a short note, and handed it to Saul: *I don't trust him, and I think this is all being recorded I'll tell you why later.*

Saul nodded and looked towards an old radio set on the rather ornate side table near where they were sitting. He wrote on the back of the note and handed it back. Alan read it and put the note in his pocket and they waited until Hobbs returned with his passport.

Alan asked, "Where is Charlie now?"

"He is at work, won't be back 'til about six. Are you not going to see me off as well, Mr Catchpole?"

"No, I am afraid I have to return to the office, my detective inspector will guard you until you are safely on the train. Alan, I will take a bus back to HQ. I am needed there. I'll let myself out and give me a call if anything changes."

Saul picked up his briefcase and left, and once out in the street again walked towards a main road where he knew he could get a bus. He waited for almost ten minutes until one arrived and got on, having searched his pockets for some change but had to pay for his fare with a £5 note. The driver gave him a rather exasperated look but issued him with a ticket.

The lower area of the bus was rather crowded so Saul went up to the top deck and sat at the rear of the bus. There were several school children with a few adults. Saul tried to remember when he had last travelled on a bus and realized it had been some years ago. In the seat four rows ahead of him was a small, very chubby boy with glasses who was gazing out of the window. Three much larger boys came up the stairs and immediately headed towards the little boy, and two sat on the seat in front and one sat next to him. Initially Saul assumed they were friends, but then he saw the small boy was looking very nervous and was trapped in his seat. One of the older boys said, "Look who we have here, lads, it's little fatty. We had his brother last week and now he's going to give us his phone and his money or he knows what will happen, don't you, Worm, or should I say, Slug!"

The small boy said, "I haven't got no money, nor have I got a phone, so I can't give you anything."

"I don't believe you, you little arse wipe, give me what you have, or I'll get these two to take your trousers and whatever you have in your pockets!"

The older boy thrust his hand into the boy's jacket and said, "You little liar, you do have a phone."

The boy handed the phone to one of the others in the seat ahead and then hit the small boy across the face quite hard, causing a nose bleed and the little lad started to cry.

Saul could see a mature lady just ahead turn to see what was going on and all the other passengers were pointedly looking out of the windows trying to pretend they did not see or hear what was happening. Saul, who stood at well over six foot, stood up and approached the group and said, "Give this lad his phone back, now!"

"Or what, you old man, mind your own business." The boy stood and suddenly produced a large hunting knife and threatened Saul with it and lunged towards him. "Get out of my way, you nosy bastard, mind your own business!"

The other two older boys were standing behind Saul. Saul noticed the mature lady moving out of her seat to assist him, and very quickly and with a degree of expertise, he grabbed the boy's hand, twisted the knife out of it and put him in an arm lock. He pushed the other two boys into the seat beside them and said to the lady, "Please ring that bell twice, and then go and tell the driver to drive straight to the nearest police station, in New Road, round the corner. I am a police officer and I am arresting these three."

The lady nodded, and did exactly as she had been asked, and two more older men at the back of the bus came up and held the two lads in their seats. The little boy was sitting in his seat looking terrified. The lady came back up the stairs, and said, "We're almost there."

She sat beside the little boy and said, "It's all right, sweetheart, you are safe now."

The larger boy was struggling to try and get out of the grip Saul had on him. The bus stopped, and in what seemed no time at all two uniformed policemen came rushing up the stairs and Saul recognized one of them.

"Mr Catchpole, sir, what's up?"

"I am arresting these three for robbery, and this one for assault with intent to rob. This little lad is the victim and these two gentlemen, and this lady, have assisted me. Have you cuffs? Good and once we have got into the station, I want details of everyone on the bus before it leaves."

Together they handcuffed the now very violent boy Saul was holding and the two men helped the uniformed officers take the boys down the stairs, and Saul frog-marched the now spitting and swearing boy after them. The lady brought the little boy and they thanked the driver as they got off the bus and they all went into the police station.

The lady said, "Can I stay with this young man, at least until someone can look after him?"

Saul still struggling to hold the youth said, "Indeed, madam, I would be most grateful for your help. I think he would too. I am very glad you were there."

The lady smiled and said, "And I that you were. Shall I wait in this front office for you?"

Two policemen came, and assisted Saul and they went into the station and through to the custody area. The custody sergeant was an officer Saul had served with in the past and knew rather well. He looked at Saul and said, "Who does the blood on the floor belong to, sir?"

"I think that might be mine, Frank. Have you an evidence bag? I have taken a knife off this boy, and I think he managed to get me in the arm as I did so. The knife is in my jacket pocket, if you could remove it. Thanks. I have arrested this boy for armed robbery and assault with intent to rob, and I suppose we shall have to add resisting arrest as well. The other two just coming in were part of it and I have also arrested them for robbery." Saul turned to the three lads and cautioned them.

The sergeant turned to the boys and the officers holding them and said, "You are now going to be searched and then I will explain what happens next."

The three lads were taken down a corridor and Frank turned to Saul and said, "Right, sir, before you tell me the circumstances would you mind not bleeding all over my floor and let this officer have a look at your wound. No, don't tell me it is nothing. I have already alerted the police surgeon and I would like him to tell me what treatment you need. He was already in the building. I understand a little boy was hurt. Where is he?"

After a few minutes the boy, the lady and Saul were ushered into an interview rom. Saul introduced himself and soon the doctor came in and checked the little lad over and then turned to Saul, and rather shortly ushered him into an adjoining office and told him to take off his jacket and examined the two inch cut just above the wrist. After cleansing the wound an officer took photographs and then the doctor fixed two steri-strips to it before binding it.

Saul asked, "Is the little boy all right, poor little chap? He got hit quite hard before I could get to him."

"Just a bit of bruising and he may have a black eye. The nose bleed has stopped. I expect they are taking photos now and contacting his next of kin. The lady is still with him. I am more concerned about you. Did he get you anywhere else?"

"No, I am fine. It was just a nick, and yes I am up to date with anti-tetanus and all that. It is not the first time I have had an injury on duty."

A few minutes later Saul joined the little boy and the lady and a WPC in the interview room. The boy rushed up to him and grasped his hand and said, "Thank you, sir, thank you. Will I be able to get my phone back?"

Saul sat down and said, "Yes, we have it safe. Jonathan isn't it? I am Mr Catchpole and I am a police officer, and I saw and heard what happened, and you are now safe. Madam, I cannot tell you how grateful I am for your help and support. Do you need to be off? We could contact you later if you are in a hurry, Mrs Hollingsworth is it?"

"I was only going to do some casual shopping. It can wait. I'll stay until his mother gets here. I think an officer has gone to fetch her?"

"Yes, that is being done. Will you be a witness?"

"Too right I will! Come on, Jonathan, why not sit with me a for a while, so the poor detective can move about a bit?"

Jonathan stared up at Saul and said, "Are you really a detective?"

"Yes, I am."

"An important one?"

"Senior, yes, not necessarily important." Saul showed the boy, and then the lady, his warrant card.

The boy looked up and said, "Do you catch murderers and that?"

"Sometimes. Yes, but today I caught three robbers."

"Cor, who?"

"Those three boys. Are they at your school?"

"Oh them, they used to be, but they are at the big school now. They is the school bullies. Is that what they were doing, robbing? I thought robbers had guns and masks and things."

"Not always. It won't be long before your mum gets here. How old are you?"

"I was eight last month. Them three are either thirteen or fourteen. They used to go to my school. They beat my brother up last week, took his pocket money. He's fourteen."

"How come you were on your own?"

"I'd been to see my gran. She's in a wheelchair. She put me on the bus and Mum was meeting me at the bus station. Can I sit on your lap?"

"If you like, for a little while. Have you got a dad?"

"I did have but he ran away. Mum says he ran away with a woman. We never see him."

"Where is your brother?"

"He's still in hospital, he's got a broken funny something and a bad bruise on the head, and he had to have a scandal or summat. They said he had a clot or was a clot."

Saul and Mrs Hollingsworth smiled at each other as they interpreted what Jonathan had said. Before long Jonathan's mother was shown in. She said to them, "Thank you so much for helping my son. Is he hurt?"

"The police surgeon says he is bruised but nothing is broken. Jonathan has been a very brave boy. I was glad I was there. May I pass you over to this officer here,

74

who will carry on for me. Jonathan, get down and give your mother a big hug, she's been very worried about you. I must go and explain to the custody officer some more things he needs to know."

Having explained everything and been assured a good officer was taking the case over, he promised a full statement by the end of the day and washed his shirt sleeve as best he could and wiped his suit. He left the station and walked the mile or so to the headquarters building. Alan was waiting for him, and Saul said, "Sorry, I got delayed."

"I heard. The enquiry officer passed on your message, and then gave me a blow by blow account. Paul told me not to let you out of my sight in future!"

"I had to do something, poor little scrap! He looked just like a mini Billy Bunter, if you are not too young to know what I am on about. I hate bullies!"

"Yes, I know. I read the books and even remember an old black and white film. Simon Hobbs got off safely and he says you are adorable!"

"Don't even think about calling me 'ducky'. You might not live long enough to repeat it, sweet pea!"

"Mum's the word, sir."

"Make sure it is. Now, let's go get Tom Cantone."

"We might have a problem. He gave the officers the slip, so I immediately went and got a warrant for his place and Anita Jones' place. They have begun the searches already. He was heading for the airport. The other team is still on Anita, she is heading there too. I took the liberty of warning them at the airport and they will hold him providing they can find him."

"Bother, so we will have to just sit and wait. Send the search teams in then."

"I already have, sir. The forensic lads say they have found some gloves, that they think may have been used to make the axe thing, hidden in an old shed in the garden of Cantone's house. Oh, and Geoff Bickerstaff rang, and said he wanted to come back to work. I said you would ring him but wanted him to take a week's leave anyway. I hope I did the right thing."

"You did, good man. Until we find Cantone I might just as well write out my statement for these three kids."

"I'll get Nita to organize a coffee. White, no sugar, isn't it?"

"You do pick things up fast, yes please."

"I also took the liberty of getting you a chicken sandwich from the canteen. I've had lunch."

"Bless you, Alan, you and I are going to work together very well, I can see that. My main regret is that in a couple of years you will move on."

"Not necessarily, sir. I am not over ambitious. Once I am settled in the right job, I doubt I will want to leave it."

"Why did you want this post anyway? I know you said all the right things on the board, but I think there is more to it than that."

"Yes, sir, there was. I've always tried to be good at what I do, not just adequate. I actually care, you see. I suppose my major sin is that of pride. I transferred for promotion, yes, but then I heard about your record and I thought if anyone could teach me, you could!"

"Flattery, however sincere will get you nowhere."

"I know that, but you asked, and I have told you."

"I make dreadful mistakes sometimes."

"Not that I've heard of and everyone makes mistakes. You seem to have a sort of intuition that I need to learn."

"I don't think you can teach that; it is something you may be born with and can develop. Look can you round up all the faxes and statements and make sure we have them all filed?"

"Already done, sir. Nita is very on the ball and you need to get on with your statement."

Saul finished the statement, faxed a copy to the custody officer and put the original in the internal post basket.

He was finishing his sandwich when Nita appeared at his office door. "Sir, the chief on the line for you."

Saul was furious when the chief explained that he had received a complaint about Saul. One of the bus passengers had deemed him rude and aggressive and hard on three poor little lads, just because they were having a bit of fun. Saul immediately took a copy of his statement to the chief, in his office. Having heard the exact nature of the complaint, he said, "Look, sir, I had every right to tell those who witnessed it that they should be ashamed of themselves. Most of the adults on the bus were deliberately ignoring a blatant case of bullying, and indeed robbery. Who has made this complaint anyway?"

"A Ms. Yvonne Salter-Hicks, a social worker who was sitting on the top of the bus. She insists that you interfered with a private laugh between friends!"

"Some friends! The little boy has bruises and those 'friends' put his brother in hospital for a week recently. I think we need to call this so-called social worker as a witness. Some social worker! It is not only ridiculous, it isn't true!"

"All right, keep your hair on, Saul. I will get it investigated properly."

"Oh, please do. I warn you, if she has made a false allegation, I shall take her to the cleaners. I will be taking advice on this, believe me. One of the women on the bus, who did help, was telling me this is quite a common occurrence on buses, and no one ever seems to do anything about it. She was very grateful that I did and says she will back me. Does no one care about victims anymore?"

"It would seem so. Has it occurred to you that these adults were themselves scared of these thugs?"

"No, they were scared of getting involved, that's all, and of their lives being inconvenienced, no more. The person who was scared was a little boy, the victim. I could no more stand by than I could fly. I've a good mind to make a complaint to the director of Social Services about the woman's inaction, in fact I think I will."

"Saul, calm down. If you must start an interdepartmental row then I can't stop you, but how will it help? What were you doing on a bus anyway?"

"My DI and I got split up. I was just getting back to the office. It seemed the easiest option."

"The other thing this woman alleged is she says you were getting a free ride and were not a fee-paying passenger." The chief visibly winced as he saw Saul getting redder in the face.

"She WHAT! Oh, good I've got her! She is simply out to make false allegations and out to make trouble, I'm not sure why. I have the ticket I purchased, in my wallet here. I paid for it with a fiver and I am sure the driver will remember it. He was very polite as he gathered the change. As a matter of interest has this woman complained about police before?"

"Many times, so I have been informed. She is a persistent complainer and there is a file on her which I am getting brought to me now. Apparently, she has, this year, made seven complaints about officers and all but one were found utterly groundless, and the other one was simply her word against the officer. Saul, please calm down, must you stir up a hornet's nest?"

"Yes, I think I must. I think it is time she learned that sometimes we can bite back. Please serve me the relevant discipline papers and let's run with it. If she thinks she can allege what she likes, and we will roll over every time I shall counter allege once I have a copy of her statement."

"All right if you must. Most officers are too worried to make a thing of it and are just happy to be off the hook when it cannot be proved."

"I'm not most officers. These are the officers who have taken on the case, and they have a whole list of those who were willing to make statements about what happened."

"OK, but now I have to find an officer senior to you to look into the matter, that is not going to be easy. From what I know, there are few senior to you who would take it on. Can I take the ticket as an exhibit? I will give you a receipt and a photocopy of it."

Chapter Five

A few minutes later Saul walked purposefully back to his office, shut the door and then rang a solicitor friend of his, and having discussed the allegation with him, then rang the Superintendent's Association and told them what had occurred. The man he spoke to had somewhat placated him telling him they already had a complaint from the same woman that they had investigated and the officer, another superintendent, had been proved to be totally innocent of any wrong doing but had declined to take civil action against the woman as he had more important family matters to attend to.

Saul sat back after the call and thought things through, in a somewhat calmer manner, and then went into the general office and noticed everyone was avidly getting on with their work and there were obviously several officers out on enquiries, which had not been the case half an hour before. No one seemed to want to catch his eye and Saul began to chuckle. "All right, everyone, I'm not angry at you at all. I wouldn't be that unjust. Alan, what is the news on Cantone?"

"Still no trace, sir. Anita Jones is waiting to board a plane to Lisbon. She just booked it. There is still plenty of time before it leaves, in fact the plane has not yet landed at the airport, so we have had time to set up a net to catch her and anyone else trying to do a bunk. If he shows as I suspect he will, we have him. We have traced his car to one of the long stay car parks there, that is being watched, as is she. She has received three calls on her mobile and has made two. Both were overheard by the team and were to him."

"Right, well done! Anything else?"

"The pathologist rang, and she says nothing unexpected has come up. Sir, did you know you have what appears to be a rather large greasy stain on the lapel of your jacket?"

"Yes, I did. It's where a little boy was eating a bun on my lap, and I think dribbling. I'll get changed in a minute. I shall obviously have to get the suit cleaned. You are on the ball, well done. Right team, come and sit down and let's go through what we know, and I could do with your input please."

While Saul went to his office and gathered up some paperwork, the rest of the squad fetched what they had, and armed themselves with coffee and soft drinks and sat round the very large table in the centre of the office. Alan had wondered why it was there and looked very surprised. He said to one of the officers, "What is going on?"

"We do this from time to time, it helps us think things out. This way everyone has their say, and it helps us to see the whole picture, not just what we ourselves are tasked with. Be prepared to take notes."

Nita armed everyone with paper and Saul sat down and joined the group. He turned to Alan and said, "Alan, we do this quite often, and I find it very helpful. Everyone gets to comment and observe. I like to know what the team think, and they often pick upon what I may have missed. I value the opinions and judgements of everyone on the squad. It means we identify gaps both in our knowledge but also in the accounts and it is a bit like constructing a large jigsaw. OK, Nita, would you start please?"

"Yes, sir. We still have several witnesses to see, that's where some of the team are now. A lot of the orchestra, but I rang the musical director, and everyone we haven't seen is coming in tomorrow morning to make a statement. One of the stage hands is coming in to see me in an hour. She says she thinks she can place the handkerchief we found, that is it from my side."

"Thanks. What can you offer, Paul?"

"Yes, I've been thinking, and I don't understand. This whole thing was meticulously planned. Why panic now? Why are they taking off? Cantone must have known about forensics. Why keep the gloves? Yes, I know they were well hidden but what has gone so wrong that they need to do a bunk?"

"Yes, I wondered about that, sir. I think we all did. It was so clever and now, they are acting like headless chickens. Are we missing something?"

"Yes, Caroline, I think we are. I am wondering if what we are missing is something that didn't happen and should have done. Is Julia still with Cantone's wife?"

"Yes, she is taking the lady back to her mother's house, in Durham. Julia told me the woman is obviously terrified, of Cantone, she thinks, and is being very helpful. Julia should ring in soon."

"Interesting. Now, Fred, any problems in the office?"

"Not much. The press have been ringing, constantly, and won't accept a referral to the press office. Your old adversary, Andrews, seems to be the main pain in the butt. What is it between him and you?"

"A mutual dislike. He is convinced that one day I will change my spots and give him an exclusive. I won't. You have been reading all the statements that have come in, what strikes you about them?"

"I think there is something missing too. To be honest, guv, I think someone else is involved and they did not do something they should have done. They chickened out. Were they supposed to hide the false axe? And get the original one back, or hide something we have found? If so who and what? As the others say this was planned so carefully, that for it all to fall apart now means something has gone badly wrong. Until Cantone is caught, I think they think they are in grave danger. Someone else knows something vital, I am sure of it!"

Alan said, "I was wondering about Hobbs, sir. I was not convinced, and I don't think you were either. Yes, he was frightened, and those tapes could have been threats, but I felt when we were there that he was like a cat playing with a mouse. I think he is a great deal cleverer than he makes out."

"I agree. Can we check he has gone to his mother's and is there?"

"I'll do it now."

As Alan got up, three officers came into the office. Tarik Singh, a detective constable fairly new on the Squad, said, "A talk through, good, I have something to contribute. Something one of the witnesses said, got me thinking. Here, Fred, the statements I took. I need to go for a Jimmy I'll be back in a minute."

One of the other officers returning said, "Nothing exceptional from me, except I saw Hobbs' partner, Charlie Fairclough, and I'm not happy. Something is not quite right."

"How about you, Andrew?"

"I followed up on Yum-Yum's husband. He is a depot manager in Wakefield. Caroline saw Yum-Yum yesterday. He had to work; he didn't tell us anything much, at least nothing we didn't already know."

"Who saw Richard Dearkin, was that you, Paul?"

"Yes, sir. We actually know each other; we are in the same golf club. Nice chap. He was totally frank with me, and explained his marriage is now on paper only, and then told me what Cyril had said about him in that row. Cyril does not like him because he acted for Ptolemy what's his name, when his marriage to Anita broke up. He also said something rather interesting about Hobbs; said we might find his background interesting. I'll just go and check that out."

"Right now, Tarik, get a coffee and tell us what it was you wanted to say."

"I went to see the Singh family; they are really nice people. Amjit, that is the father, made me very welcome. They all made statements, nothing special in them, but after they had, Amjit started telling me a story about a great uncle of his, in the Punjab. At first, I thought he was just reminiscing, but then he explained that this uncle had been a magician, a travelling one. He was quite successful. I listened mainly to be polite, but then Amjit said his uncle had a device, rather like the axe, the murder weapon. He said it was an old magicians' trick that his uncle had picked up somewhere. The trick he used it in was to slice a watermelon, but what his uncle had was a sort of stick, that collapsed to produce a cutting edge, a blade, He then went and found an old photograph, which he gave me. I have it here. Amjit gently suggested that we look at some tricks that magicians use. He thinks the design might be similar."

"Does anyone know any magicians?"

"Yes, I do. I dealt with a case once, where a well-known one on the showbiz round, had his props stolen, by a rival, as it happens. We got them all back, and the man still comes and does the kids' parties for us at Christmas. His name is the Great Valerene, but his real name is Albert Smith. Shall I ring him?"

"Yes please, Paul. Anything else, anyone? Yes, Fred?"

"Just a little thing, sir. You took Hobbs' stage directions and libretto the night it happened. I've been looking at it. Most of it is self-explanatory but there are some odd coloured dots and strange markings on it. I don't understand, they look fresh. They only occur in the first act. I think we should find out what they mean, if only because on another copy they are not there."

"Well spotted! No, that was not meant to be a joke. What was it about Charlie that you didn't like, Colin?"

"Quite a lot, but so far as this case is concerned, there are several things. He and Hobbs have only been together about five months, and as far as Charlie is concerned it is not serious and he was already thinking of moving on. He was saying that he found out, last month, that Hobbs' real name is something else. Someone in the gay community told him, that the name is actually Dobbs, and when he was in Wolverhampton, he worked in an engineering plant, something to do with blades for some garden machinery manufacturer. They also told him he had been married at some point, and there is a child as a result. It is funny that you mentioned magic because I saw quite a lot of books on magic on the bookshelves there as well as some engineering reference books in addition to loads of scores and librettos and the like, and wait for it, two bookcases full of Mills and Boon, one of Barbara Cartland and a complete collection of Agatha Christie's. There are also books on pathology, famous murder cases and murderers and forensic science. Charlie admitted the Mills and Boon were his, and the Cartland, but not the rest, except a few art books. There were quite a few books on Japanese military history and martial arts too."

"You noticed a lot!"

"I asked to look round and Charlie let me. He's moving out. He says he has found someone else, less controlling, less sadistic, so he says. He asked I don't let Hobbs know his new address. I asked him outright if he was scared of Hobbs and he said yes."

"I think we have been taken for mugs by Hobbs. Nita, can you and Fred make enquiries under the name Dobbs? And talk to Wolverhampton. Yes, Alan, any news?"

"He's not in Bournemouth, not at his mother's anyway. She rang her daughter in Stoke on Trent, he's not been there either. His name was Dobbs. His mother married again. I've got the local CID to go round. They say they will do it asap, but she is most worried as she says she didn't know he was out!"

"Out of where?"

"Out of prison. He told her he had been caught smuggling drugs and would be away for a while. I'll get back to them and update them."

"How strange. Why tell us his mother's address if he knows we can check up on him?"

"Are we sure that it is his mother?"

"Good point, Paul. Alan, please send a photo down, get them to check. Unless Cantone turns up there is not much more we can do now, that we are not already doing. When you have finished your allotted tasks, knock off, but please stay on call. We will meet at nine in the morning. Alan, can you join me? I need to get a statement from Geoff."

"I trust you will not be taking the bus, sir?"

"Very droll, Paul. No, we will take my car. You are the late supervisor, ring me if anything occurs."

"Certainly."

As they left the office a male voice was heard to mutter, "Hold very tight please, ring ring!" followed by general laughter.

Saul chuckled and said, "Now we will have bus jokes for the next few days at least. When I first took on the squad, I interviewed a zoo keeper, he was a witness to a fatal pub stabbing. I went to see him at work, not knowing he was an elephant keeper. One of the elephants decided to shower me with elephant dung. I had to come back to change. We had elephant jokes round the squad for weeks!"

"You don't mind them taking the piss?"

"Not at all, no. It keeps the humour going, which makes the team stronger. You know what they say, if you can't take a joke…"

"You shouldn't have joined, I know. My last governor would have gone crackers, and considered it impertinent, insubordinate even."

"Which only made everyone do it behind his back, or anonymously. I would never stop it that way, just cause bad feeling. I fell off a cliff about eighteen months ago, got injured. Before I left hospital, they brought me pamphlets on hang gliding, cliff diving, rock climbing, all sorts. It made me laugh a lot, which did help. It stops me becoming pompous, too self-important. The moment they have something on you, I suggest you deal with it the same way. I won't let anyone be hassled about things that might hurt them, religious beliefs and that, and personal integrity criticism is taboo, but the rest, we can all get a bit too serious sometimes."

"I was told you were different; I'm beginning to see why. No, I can take a joke, along with the next man. I did notice the cartoons on the noticeboard, and a few framed ones on the office walls. Who does them, they are rather good?"

"I put my hands up to some of them. If they can take the mickey then so can I. Alan, we deal with horrific things, death, devastation. We have to have something to laugh about, just to relieve the horror. Most of the team have been with me some time. They are very good at it. Without them I would be lost. I may head the team, but they do most of the work."

"Yes, I realize that you all work together. These thinking sessions, you bounce off each other?"

"Yes, we use each other's brains."

"My last boss considered anyone under the rank of inspector was incapable of independent thought. He took everything on himself."

"And will soon be out on a stress related retirement, no doubt. Your role is vital, you are a keystone, you can field ideas, problems from both directions. Can you answer my phone, I must visit the gents?"

When Saul rejoined him, Alan said, "They have Cantone, and Anita Jones. They tried to board the flight at the last minute. They are bringing them back, in separate vehicles. I asked them to take her to another station, he is coming here. Did I do right?"

"Quite right. Look you take over with them, use Paul to help you. I must go and see Geoff. I'll come back as soon as I can. Will you please be the officer in the case?"

"Surely that should be you?"

"Not necessarily, I'll help of course. May I suggest you tell them as little as possible and seek a remand for both of them in custody."

"Yes, I will, we have enough to charge, certainly. I'll get the usual DNA fingerprints and all that. I expect they will want solicitors."

Saul went to see his sergeant, Geoff Bickerstaff. He took a statement from him. The man was very shaken and subdued but in control of all his faculties.

"Sir, thank you for what you did, for me and for my missus. She told me, so did my son, Jo. The new DI told me to take at least a week off, but there must be something I can do?"

"There is, Geoff. I want you to go away for a damn good holiday. It would not be appropriate for you to work on this case at all. Have you spoken to the force medical officer?"

"Yes, he came to see me with offers from the force psychiatrist and a counsellor. I am seeing them tomorrow. Thanks for fixing that up for me. If you don't need me, I'll go to France for a week."

"If you want somewhere more exotic, and haven't the funds, let me know and I will sub you."

"That is very kind of you, but we have friends in Sarlat, good friends. They rang and said to come anytime. I'll give you their address and number. If you need me for the inquest or anything I'll get back. Sir, I need to tell you, I had no idea. I didn't know, please believe me?"

"I know that, Geoff, but I will get to the bottom of it, trust me. Let me know if you need anything. I must get back as we have made two arrests."

"May I ask who?"

"Tom Cantone and Anita Jones, but we think there are more involved."

"I can't say I am that surprised. I should tell you; Tom and I fell out. He told me to mind my own business and to leave him alone."

"Yes, Geoff, I was told!"

"No, I mean he spoke to me after the row in the Green Room. He almost threatened me. Said if I crossed him, I would regret it. Told me if I went bleating to his Board of Governors, he'd see I was out of a job!"

"Did he now? How was he going to do that, did he say?"

"He said something unfortunate might happen and no one would believe I was innocent. And I would have to prove it. It has, hasn't it?"

"I see, his nasty plan has just gone a bit wrong. We know you are innocent, and I shall prove it. I'll ring you if I need you."

When Saul got back to the office, Alan said, "Neither of them wants to talk at all, they have solicitors and I will interview in the morning. They need a rest period anyway. Most of the squad have booked off. What do you need me to do?"

"The same, but if you like, follow me to my place and join us for supper?"

Chapter Six

When Saul and Alan pulled up at Saul's home, five dogs rushed out of the house to greet them, very enthusiastically. His son Stephen was there with his wife Clarissa and their baby son Benjamin, and their two dogs.

Inside the house was chaotic. Saul's brother Jake appeared from the kitchen causing much laughter as he pretended to be the chef from the Muppets. Saul's two daughters were helping him, at least that is what they said. Having calmed the dogs, Saul pulled Hercules out of the way and ushered Alan into the lounge where Anna and Clarissa were sitting.

"Clarissa, may I introduce you to Alan Withers? This is my daughter-in-law, Clarissa. Where are Stephen and Benjamin?"

"Alan, do come in. I trust Saul mentioned we have a mad house at the moment? Sit down, relax, please, I've been banished from the kitchen. It's all right, I know you are a veggie, so Jake has promised us an Indonesian meal. Is that all right?"

"Wonderful, Mrs Catchpole, thanks."

"No, dear, you call me Anna. I'm not a senior officer, if I may call you Alan?"

"Help yourself to a drink from the cabinet over here. Saul, I don't know what you have been doing, that suit needs cleaning. He comes back covered with all sorts sometimes. Once it was elephant droppings."

"Yes, he told me about that. Shall I get my jumper from the car, if we are going to be casual?"

Saul smiled and said, "Yes, do, but in this house, or when we are alone, you call me Saul, please. Before he tells you, Anna, the current jokes are about buses, not elephants."

The meal was fantastic, exotic, aromatic and tasty. There was a selection of dishes to suit everyone. Jake, as usual, sort of took over and Alan found himself crying with laughter and totally relaxed. At the end of the meal he got up and helped clear the dishes and the dining room table, with Stephen.

"Dad likes you, I can tell. Please look after him. He takes everything so seriously, almost takes the sorrows of the world on his shoulders. He also works too hard. He told me that sometimes, being in charge can be very lonely. It will help if you two can confide in each other. He won't let you down and I hope that you won't let him down."

"I won't, believe it. I think he is amazing. I've only been with him a week, and already I've learned so much. He has a brilliant sense of humour. Are these paintings by him?"

"Yes, he is a good artist. He loves hillwalking, when he can, and paints usually country scenes. Look I have banished Mum and Dad from the kitchen. Can you help me load the dishwasher?"

As they cleared the kitchen, Alan asked, "What is your line of work?"

"I run an IT firm, computer graphics mainly. Have you any family? Coming here is rather a baptism of fire. It isn't normally like this."

"It's fun. No, I have no family. I was married, but not any more. That's why I decided to move to somewhere new, make a fresh start, so to speak."

"Do you play sport at all; I might be able to introduce you to a few clubs and things like that?"

"Football, mainly, I am about average, not a bad left back. I like badminton and squash too. I will need to find a sports centre."

"I can help you there. Who do you support? I sort of follow Leeds."

"Arsenal."

While the kitchen was being put right, and the baby Benjamin was being bathed upstairs by his mother and the two young girls, Saul managed to sit down with Anna in the lounge. Anna said, "I like him he has a great sense of humour, and he almost reminds me of you when you were younger. Look, I've some rather important news to tell you. You know Great Aunt Mathilda died last month?"

"You told me. I liked the old lady a lot. You thought she would leave all she had to Ruth?"

"Well she didn't. She left her house to Ruth but the rest she has left to us, you and me."

"What? But she was fabulously wealthy, wasn't she?"

"Yes, she was. The solicitor came and saw me. Here is the letter he gave me. It means we could give up work if we wanted to. Do you?"

"No, but would you like to?"

"Yes, I would love to now there are grandchildren to look after, and I am sure I can find plenty to do."

"Well so far as I am concerned it is your money, so you do what you want. How has Ruth taken it?"

"I don't know, I think she will be furious, should we give her some?"

"Your dearest sister that hates me and our family, no I don't think so. It is up to you, but that old mausoleum must be worth a cool million, and she could sell it. She has caused enough trouble in this house, and I want nothing more to do with her. If she starts on you, tell me and I will sort it out."

"I hoped you would say that. I'm terrified she'll turn up here, accusing me of taking it from her. She always expected it all, she said she was Aunt Mattie's favorite."

"I know but on the few occasions I met the old lady she told me that she thought you were by far the nicer person. For some reason she seemed to approve of me. We can talk this through later, I think mayhem is about descend, because that sounds alarmingly like Jake singing! As Stephen cannot sing, I wonder who is joining in, it must be Alan. Oh, watch out here they come, dogs and all!"

After a while when a boisterous game ensued, apparently involving furniture in the conservatory, Saul and Alan retreated to his study.

"Saul, I love your family, they are such fun! I haven't enjoyed myself so much for ages."

"Good! Alan, did I hear you singing?"

"Yes, bad mistake. I know, your brother sort of talked me into it. It was a song we sang at school. I asked him if there was a choir I could join; I can actually manage a tenor part. He said he'd get me details. I should really make a move as I have to get back and we do have an early start. I'll just thank Anna, and say goodnight, err… what was that loud crash?"

They went into the conservatory, to find Jake, Hercules, two Labradors and Stephen in a heap on the remains of a wicker sofa and a coffee table. The two girls were on the floor nearby, convulsed with laughter. Saul waited patiently as they got up and Jake, looked at the devastation and said, "Sorry, that went a bit wrong. I think it's past mending, I will replace it."

Saul looked at the broken furniture and said, "I'll get something more sturdy, it was old anyway."

Saul pulled Alan away and the pair of them held their laughter in until they got out to the drive.

"That was hilarious, I'll see you tomorrow. Drive carefully."

As Stephen and his wife and child got ready to leave, Saul took him on one side. "Are you all right for money, son, I know babies are expensive?"

"Dad, I probably earn more than you do. No, we are fine, but I did want to ask you what you wanted for your birthday next week. I'd rather get you something you want, not another pair of socks."

"Actually, could you get me a portable easel for me to take out on walks. Mine died when some sheep trampled it a bit back."

Stephen hugged his father and said, "No problem, but please, take care of yourself. I worry about you!"

"Why?"

"You deal with murderers and that and you don't exactly have a risk-free job. I want Benjamin to know his grandad. I worry."

"All right I'll be careful, now get my sleepy grandson home!"

**

The next morning Saul was in the office early and had looked through the paperwork piled on his desk. He found an envelope from The Discipline and Complaints department, and a letter in it telling him to be available to be interviewed at noon that day. He put it aside and soon the squad room was filling up, and when the tasks had been allocated, Saul and Alan went to interview Cantone. A solicitor was present and after the introductions the solicitor said, "Mr Cantone has prepared a statement, but does not wish to answer any questions, except to clarify what he says. I will read it to you.

'I have been arrested on suspicion of murder or conspiracy to murder. This is quite unjustified. I have not killed anyone and resent the implication and accusation that I have. This whole mess is the result of a conspiracy between Cyril Jones, Geoffrey Bickerstaff and Simon Hobbs trying to frame me. When Cyril discovered that Anita and I were in love, he threatened to kill himself, and informed me that if he did so he would make sure that I would be blamed for his death. He said if he couldn't have Anita, he would make sure I

couldn't either. He was a vindictive and cruel man, who abused Anita, and we were planning to leave together after the show. Cyril asked me to be there that night, said something was going to happen that would show me he meant what he said. Then he said Geoffrey would explain, if I wouldn't listen to him. Simon Hobbs insisted I was on the stage, in the wings, when it happened. Simon lies about most things, so you won't get the truth from him. Whatever evidence you think you have against me will have been planted by Bickerstaff and Jones with a hand from Simon. I was horrified at what happened. I see that things look black for me, but I am innocent. I wanted to get Anita away from it all, and once she was safe abroad, I was going to return to clear my name. Simon rang me, told me you were coming to arrest me, he was enjoying what he said. Anita and I arranged to meet at the airport. She is, as I am, innocent of everything except falling in love with each other. You may want to know why they disliked me so much as to conspire to frame me. Cyril was jealous and wanted to humiliate Anita and keep her, and he wanted to punish me. Bickerstaff is a self-righteous rather boring flat-footed policeman, who thought he had the right to preach morality to me. He didn't like it when I told him to mind his own business. Hobbs is a disgusting little pervert with a power fixation, who I always despised, and he hated me for saying so. I expect, therefore, to be released immediately and I will be lodging a complaint about my treatment and expect considerable compensation for the damage to my reputation!'

"That is Mr Cantone's statement. He assures me of his total innocence."

"Thank you, Mr Farmer. Shall we clarify a few things? Mr Cantone, were there any witnesses to these conversations you had with Bickerstaff and Jones?"

"No, they would hardly say anything like that in company."

"When and where did these conversations take place?"

"The first one with Cyril was in the car park after the dress rehearsal. The second one was again in the car park, on opening night, just before the show. Simon Hobbs asked me twice to be on stage. Once after the opening night that was in the Green Room, just after the show, and again on the backstage stairs, the night before it happened. Whenever possible, I tried to avoid Bickerstaff, and I think him me."

"Did you make the false axe, the murder weapon?"

"No."

"Did you suggest to Flavia Baker that the mock execution was inserted?"

"Yes."

"Why?"

"I thought it would add to the drama."

"You gave the design of the axe to Flavia?"

"Simon Hobbs gave it to me to give to her."

"Your house and premises have been searched. Here is a copy of the warrant. We can forensically prove that the axe was made in your tool shed and a pair of gloves found hidden there were in contact with that axe. How do you explain that?"

"Obviously planted there by one or all of the three of them."

"Have you ever worn those foundry gloves?"

"Not that I know of, I don't know what you are talking about."

"The real props axe was also in contact with those gloves. How do you explain that?"

"Same answer, they were planted."

"This warrant also requires you to provide us with a DNA sample, which will be compared with those gloves. Are you still saying you know nothing about these gloves? "

Cantone paused and looked at his solicitor and then said, "No reply."

"Once we have your DNA profile it will of course be compared to a database. Is it going to match any other name?"

"Of course not, I've never been in any sort of trouble with the police, ever."

"That is not quite true. You have never been convicted but you were investigated for tampering with a motor vehicle belonging to a Kevin Evans."

"That was a malicious fabrication too. I had to tell him off and he made an untruthful allegation about me."

"The samples that were taken at the time are still stored, that case is still active, and when your profile is compared to them, what will it tell us? Do you wish to make any comment?"

"No."

"You say in your statement that is was only in the last couple of days that you decided to leave the country with Anita, and that the decision was made after Cyril died?"

"That's right."

"Then how do you explain that the tickets were booked in the names of Mr and Mrs Smith, with your credit card six weeks ago?"

"No comment."

"If you are innocent, as you claim, why did you avoid speaking to us? You lied about being required to go to the school. An innocent man would have wanted to explain his innocence."

"No comment."

"I believe you have a degree in engineering from Salford University?"

"Yes."

"What kind of engineering?"

"That is my business. No comment."

"What is your financial situation?"

"No comment."

"Do you have a property in the Algarve?"

"No comment."

"You allege the evidence was planted in your shed. When did you last go into the shed?"

"No comment."

"Have you ever been in a production where a fatal accident took place before?"

"No."

"How many times have you been in Ruddigore?"

"Twice, both with this society."

"I believe it was your first production with this society?"

"Yes, it was."

"When you auditioned then, you told the casting committee you had already been in one production of Ruddigore."

"I was bullshitting."

"So you are not the Tom Bell who was in Ruddigore at Salford University, when a fatal accident occurred to Alistair Cotton, who was playing the part of Richard Dauntless?"

"No."

"I have here the programmes of your first production of Ruddigore with the society, and here I have the programme of the Salford University production. The part of Sir Despard Murgatroyd was played by you, with this society. Is that your photograph?"

"Yes, it says so, doesn't it?"

"Now compare the photograph of Tom Bell who played the same part at Salford. I would say that is not only you, it is the same photograph."

Cantone looked at the two photographs and so did his solicitor.

"No comment."

The solicitor said, "Can I confer with my client please?"

"Certainly, I am suspending the interview."

Saul and Alan left the room and got a cup of coffee from the machine while they waited to be called back into the room. After a while the solicitor came out and said, "He does not want to talk about that and will not do so. I take it, it is relevant?"

"Very. We will leave that until later. Shall we resume, or do you want a coffee before we do so?"

The solicitor accepted the offer and when they had drunk their coffees the interview was resumed and once again Cantone was cautioned.

"Mr Cantone, at your school on your desk, we found a handwritten note. On it is the speech you gave to the audience after Cyril Jones was killed. It is, word for word, what you said. How do you explain that?"

"I wrote it afterwards. I needed to tell you what had happened and what I said."

"So when did you put it there?"

"The evening after it happened. I went into school about seven o'clock, after the caretaker had gone home. I have a set of keys."

"Are you sure?"

"Yes of course I am."

"No, at that time on that evening, and for several hours either side of that time you were in the company of Anita Jones, at the Boars Head Pub, Threshfield, and after that you went to the White Hart Hotel."

"No, you are mistaken."

"We can prove it."

"How?"

"At least three officers were watching you and Mrs Jones. You booked in under the name of Mr and Mrs Smith and left about ten that night."

"What right had you to watch me?"

"I am sure you will discuss this with Mr Farmer here. I suggest you have a re-think, and come up with something to convince us that you are as innocent as you claim."

"I am innocent."

"Quite frankly Mr Cantone, or Mr Bell, I don't believe you and I don't think a jury will either. Stop lying to us, you are not very good at it. When you have had a re-think, we will talk again. Interview terminated time, 10.30 a.m."

Alan and Saul went straight down to the other police station where Caroline and Paul had just finished their interview with Anita.

Alan said, "How did you two get on with her?"

"She's like a terrified rabbit. Came up with a cock and bull story about their being set up by Cyril. The story is full of holes. It won't take much to crack her next time. We did get something unexpected though. She has been married four times. Her first married name was Dobbs. I didn't push it, just made out it was routine to check dates, places."

"Very interesting. Is she a bit thick?"

"Yes, but also a bit sly. If she had any sign of sorrow over her husband's death, she is hiding it well. The WPC who searched her came and found us. She had quite a bit of money, mainly euros, hidden in her underwear, about ten grands' worth. She also had an E111 card, as well as her passport."

"So how long did she say she had them?"

"She admitted six weeks or more, told us Tom Cantone told her to get it. In her property she also had a load of euro cheques and an American Express card. Her cases were packed for a long stay, and a number of things spoke of forward planning, such as adaptors, a Portuguese/English dictionary, a Linguaphone Portuguese course, swim wear, sunblock, and diarrhea pills. All purchased six weeks ago. The silly woman still had the receipts in her case."

Alan said, "There was quite a bit in Cantone's cases too. His health card, his bank details in Portugal, a branch in the Algarve."

Saul sighed. "Oh dear she isn't acting very bright, is she? How would you describe her, Caroline?"

"Very bimboesque, dumb blonde, the WPC also mentioned she thought she was pregnant. The doctor is checking her out now. The WPC also suggested the bimbo bit was an act, and she is a lot brighter than she is making out."

"Who is this WPC?"

"A Sandra Lancashire. She is acting up in the cells as custody officer."

"Sandra is probably right, she is a very clever woman. I know her. Can you ask her to pop in and see me? Look I must go, I am being interviewed by an ACC from Derbyshire Complaints and Discipline at noon, which should be interesting if nothing else."

Alan said, "OK I will warn everyone to be out of the office then…"

"Why, he won't mind your being in the office?"

"No, for when you come out. Sod him minding, none of us want to be around when you are angry."

"Paul, that's not fair!"

"It is to us, we don't want the gimlet eyes and the scowl, thanks, sir."

"I don't, do I?"

"Occasionally, when you are cross. We just try to keep out of the way until you calm down."

"I'm sorry, I never realized. I won't take it out on you lot."

"You won't get the chance, sir, good luck!"

Saul did not know whether to be cross or amused. Back in his office he was waiting with his friend and superintendent colleague, Wally Evans, when the ACC came in. There was another man with him who was introduced as Inspector Grey. Saul politely offered his chair to the Assistant Chief Constable, who said to Wally, "You can go now."

Saul said, "This is my superintendent representative and I wish him to stay, and I have a right to do so. You have this officer with you and I would insist on one too. If you cannot accept that I have rights too, then this interview stops right now. I am also recording the whole thing and will be delighted to give you a copy of the tape at the end of the interview."

"I was told you would be difficult. Here are the discipline papers, just sign them and give them back please."

"Certainly, I'll just read them first. I never sign anything without first reading it carefully. Yes, these seem to be in order."

"Right, let's hear your side of the story then."

Wally said, "I think before anything else you need to caution Mr Catchpole."

"Oh, for goodness sake, it isn't as if he doesn't know the caution!"

Wally sighed. "Let's do this correctly or not at all, please. I see you have a copy of a statement that I presume was made by the complainant, please may we see exactly what she alleges, and any other evidence you have. I will copy them. I take it you have no objection."

"If you must?"

Saul read the statement through twice before he said, "May I now invite you to read the statements taken from the other witnesses, the officers dealing with the robbery, the custody officer, and from my chief constable, to whom I gave the bus ticket for my journey that I had purchased. I also include a statement taken by a colleague from the bus driver in which he states that I paid with a five-pound note. I think that is included in the evidence as well. Here is my pocket book which I would be grateful if you would time and date, and the copies of all the other relevant pocket books and evidence. The statement from the boy who was the victim and his mother are there too."

The ACC read through all the evidence and passed it to his side kick. "That certainly puts a different slant on things. Now, have you any answers to her allegations?"

"Yes I do. She complains that I was rude. I was not rude. Although I did say to those who should have done something that they should be ashamed of themselves. She then says I blasphemed. I invite you to see what I actually said in those statements. I do not blaspheme. She says I said, 'Fucking Christ', which I never would say. I do not swear."

"We all swear at times."

Wally chipped in. "Actually, I have never heard Saul swear, and I have known him and worked with him for many years. He certainly wouldn't say that."

"You have never sworn like that?"

"Well I wouldn't take the name of Christ in vain, no and I did not use the 'f' word."

"Are you a serious Christian then?"

"No I am Jewish, and it is a matter of principle that I do not offend other religions."

"I was also told you were a bit different. What else will you say about her allegations?"

"The facts really speak for themselves. She states here, 'He wouldn't have paid for his fare, police officers never do. I'm sure he never paid.' My reply to that is as she was already on the bus upstairs, she would not have seen me get on, or purchase the ticket. As a matter of interest, you may not know but the bus company invites officers on duty to travel on their buses free of charge, they are grateful for a uniform presence."

"So what you are saying is that if you had shown your warrant card you could have travelled free?"

"Probably, but as I was in civvies, I preferred to pay my fare. I don't take freebies or abuse an agreement like that. That is a false allegation by her that I can disprove and casts a different light on the rest of what she says. At the time she said nothing, did nothing, and denied seeing anything at all. Now she has a lot to say. I invite you to look at the records we have for the three boys who I arrested on the bus for robbery. All have come to notice before and have ASBOs. The boys' mother thinks they beat up her elder son because she helped the authorities in a obtaining those ASBOs. Her elder boy is still in hospital after their assault on him."

"I see, they are not the little angels she makes out, are they? I spoke to Ms. Salter-Hicks, she says she will accept a public apology from you, if we reach an informal resolution."

"Well she won't get one. I want the whole matter formally dealt with and investigated. Then I will take whatever legal action against her that is appropriate."

"Is it worth it?"

"It is to me. I take it you have seen her record for previous complaints made against officers?"

"Yes, I have. This could blow up, be very damaging, drawn out. Had you considered that?"

"Of course I have, sir. Her complaint is against me personally. It is false, malicious, and she chose to make it. Let her try to prove it. Someone has to stand up to troublemakers like her, at some time. I am the first to admit if I make mistakes and apologize for them. I will accept just criticism. If I am out of order, I would expect to de be disciplined. If I am in the right, however, as I know I am in this instance, I will not accept a spiteful attempt to knock my Office of Constable, or the reputation of the Force. I will not give way on this, sir, believe me."

"Oh I do. It does seem to be a malicious and fictitious complaint, and when that is proved are you intending to take it further?"

"Once your enquiry is complete, I have already instructed a solicitor to look at suing her for libel."

"You can't do that?"

Wally said, "I have taken legal advice on this too, and yes, he can. He has the full backing of the Superintendent's Association on this."

"I see. Are you normally this difficult?"

"According to those close to me and my team, yes. Look, without trying to prejudice the issue can I offer you and this gentleman some refreshment? I know you have come some way."

"Thanks but no, we will go to the canteen. I must contact this Sgt Pepper, is that really his name?"

"Yes, sir. I can get him to ring you."

"No, just give him my number. Have you a number I may contact you on, if I need to speak to you again? Thanks, a card."

"Here, sir, copies of the tape. Now allow me to escort you to the senior officers' dining room. Saul, go and get on with this murder enquiry."

Wally went out of the office with the two visitors and Saul went into an almost deserted squad room. The only people there were Nita, Fred and the typist Janice. They immediately seemed to be engrossed in their work. Saul felt just a little hurt. Then Saul saw a series of new pictures stuck to the walls of the room and went over and examined them. The three heads went down again. The pictures were of a collection of buses. Saul read one of the captions and roared with laughter.

"It's all right; tell the others it is safe to come back. Who contributed this one, it's brilliant, a wonderful skit of a Flanders and Swann song, 'Hold very tight please'? It is very witty. Who was it?"

"I believe that was DI Withers, sir."

"Good, I must compliment him. Now, where is everyone?"

"Having lunch, sir."

"Have you lot eaten?"

"Not yet, sir."

"Then go, I will remain until the others get back."

Fred paused by the door and said, "How did it go, sir?"

"Much as expected. Go get your lunch!"

When Alan returned, Saul smiled at him and said, "Thanks for the Flanders and Swann sketch, it cheered me up no end. Now, update me."

"Cantone wishes to amend his statement. His solicitor will be there at two p.m. Anita Jones wants to talk again, wishes to confess her part in it. Hobbs has turned up in Rochdale of all places. He is now being watched. Charlie told me where to look. We have done some more checks, well Nita has, and it seems that Anita and Hobbs were married, albeit briefly. It's all getting very interesting, have you had lunch?"

"I'm not very hungry."

"Are you all right?"

"I suppose so."

"Can I help?"

"No, I don't think so. I think I had evidence to prove she is an out and out liar. What is this letter?"

"Oh, that came just before lunch. Hand delivered, for you."

Saul opened it and showed it to Alan.

Dear Mr Catchpole,

Thank u somuch for helping me. Me mum says tahns to. My armis beter now. karl cums home today from Hosptal. I fink u is wonderful. I wantto be a copper when I grows up.

Luv, Jonathan.

Alan smiled and said, "I think this should go on the case file."

"Maybe. You know, that makes me feel that it was all worthwhile. Poor kid was terrified. Every year at Christmas we have a Christmas party for children who have come to our attention in some way, kids who have helped, been brave or victims, you know, winner of school competitions or scouts and the like. I'll make sure he, and his brother are invited."

The second interview with Cantone was much more revealing. After the introductions, Cantone, in a much less pompous manner, said, "Look, I was lying earlier.

About a lot of things. I know you can prove it too. I will admit what I have done. I think I know I am going down for a long time, so I might just as well tell you the truth."

"Please do, where do you want to start?"

"At the beginning. You are quite right, I used to be Tom Bell. My real name is actually Thomas Campanile, Italian for bell tower. My parents changed all our names when I was about ten. I went, as you said to Salford University, got a degree in structural engineering. That production of Ruddigore scared me. It was a genuine accident that happened, but I never forgot it. I was a bit of a womanizer at the time, but I eventually settled down, and took up teaching."

"Were you married at that point?"

"No, I got promoted, moved around a bit, met my wife in an operatic society and although we never had kids, we were happy for a while, and then things changed. We started falling out, usually over silly things. You mentioned Kevin Evans. You know why I hated him?"

"Because you suspected he was seeing your wife?"

"I knew he was. He was really a rather unpleasant chap and delighted in rubbing my nose in it. Yes, I tampered with his brakes when his bike was outside my house and he was screwing my missus. I am only admitting it now because I cut my finger and you will probably have blood or at least DNA. He then left the area and it blew over, but I knew she was seeing many other men and quite frankly I no longer cared. I had been in this operatic society for a while and then Anita joined. For some reason she fancied Cyril, although I did try then to attract her, but I didn't have the money he did. At the time she was divorcing poor Ptolemy, and I know he still cares for her. She married Cyril, but he is no fool. He knew what she was like and I don't think she was very happy that Cyril wanted to control her every move and expected her to keep house and be the little woman at home. About this time Hobbs turned up, and it was obvious they knew each other. He is paid, you know, and he is very good at what he does. By this time Ptolemy was off the scene and she turned to me. I do love her, very much."

"Tell me about the barbeque at your place, when some people got ill."

"I'll come to that, don't worry, Anita told me that she and Simon had been married once. She said a marriage of convenience, for both of them. Her to get out of a sticky situation and him so he could inherit money left to him, by an uncle on condition he did marry. They had parted after the minimum time, on good terms. Each free to go their own way, but five months later she realized she was pregnant. Neither wanted the child, so it was adopted. Her next marriage only lasted a short time: he was violent. He was a musician. Then she met Ptolemy, and he was not well off and she wanted a better life, obviously offered by Cyril. He was not what she thought, and he was no fool either. I admit I was jealous, and she was always telling me he was mean and wouldn't let her live the way she wanted. The only time he would let her out was to come to the operatic society, about which he was fanatical. She knew if she left him, she would get nothing as he had tied all his considerable wealth up in a prenuptial agreement. If we married, I would have to give my wife our home which left me with my place in the Algarve. I am not rich.

"Anita's adopted child tracked her down and wanted to meet her. She had never told Cyril about the kid, and Simon said he would talk to him, but he didn't really want to know. My wife was away so they met the lad at my place. They talked for some time and then he left. Simon said he would deny him and the three of us got talking. Simon suggested this way out, to get rid of Cyril, she would inherit, and we could all live the lives we wanted. I laughingly told them about the thing in Ruddigore where that chap died and said wasn't it a shame that there couldn't be an accident like that."

"Was Simon with Charlie then?"

"Yes, but I was told it was only a flirtation. Simon came round several times and it always ended by talking about how Cyril could have a fatal accident. Then about two months ago he came up with this plan. He had it all worked out, all he said he wanted was a share of the money. He even produced sketches of the axe and explained how it would work. He told us two to cool off for a bit. He then told me to suggest the mock execution to Flavia."

"Why?"

"I'm not sure. I know he had a bit of a hold over Flavia, and he said she would listen to me. She thought it was a wonderful bit of drama. I offered to make the prop axe, but Jeanette was asked to do that. I made the folding one to a detailed plan given me by Simon. I had to 'borrow' the prop on for a couple of days to make sure they looked identical. Simon got it for me and put it back. There was quite a difference in weight, so I think he put some weight on to the prop one. It was Simon's plan to get Anita to swop the axes and he gave her a handkerchief to use while handling it. I've been thinking about that. Somewhere I heard that the Japanese did not use handkerchiefs at all. It might be somewhere in the libretto, I think. Simon did insist I was there early that night, in case Anita fell apart and he said my being there would help. He also told me to prepare that speech which would give him time to sort any last-minute glitches out."

"That was when you went front stage, after the curtain came down and told everyone not to panic, and there had been an accident?"

"Yes. I had to step over Cyril's head to get to front of stage. It was very grizzly."

"Who made the false chopping block?"

"Simon, I think. Anyway it all went to plan. Simon was going to hide the false axe, and said all the evidence would be gone by the time you lot got there."

"But he didn't!"

"No he didn't. He did nothing and by the time I realized he had set us up it was too late. I don't think he even wanted the money. Anita thinks it was done out of spite."

"So why, then?"

"Jealousy, spite; he can't forgive her for divorcing him, hatred, putting the kid up for adoption. I was just the patsy who was in love with her and he used both of us. And like idiots we panicked and tried to get away. When you saw me earlier, I realized I had been set up and now I think it is best for the truth to come out. Oh, and I gave the gloves to Simon and he said he would get rid of them. He must have put them and some other stuff back in my shed. I actually made the axe in the house, not the shed."

"You admit plotting the murder then?"

"Yes, I do. But you have to believe me, Simon was the mastermind. He planned it, including, I suspect, getting me and Anita to take the blame. He pulled us into his devious little trap. After it happened, and I saw what we had done I was horrified. I think I was almost convinced it would never work or he wouldn't do it."

"I am told you had a hold over Flavia. What hold?"

"She is a convicted shoplifter. I just happened to find out when I went to the courts one day to speak for one of the children. I was in the public gallery."

"Why did you press for Flavia to be Katisha?"

"Mainly because I am not that keen on coppers and Julia is far too observant and clever."

"Is Geoff Bickerstaff innocent?"

"Of course he is, utterly. I actually feel very sorry for him. He is the straightest chap I know. I am sorry I lied about him; he was just a necessary tool in Simon's plot. Will you tell him I am sorry? I do know that Simon does not like him at all."

"I will. Now, I cannot offer you a deal, but would you be prepared to give evidence about this?"

"Yes, I will. I know I am no better and in effect just as guilty, but I don't see why Anita and I should take all the blame when he gets off scot-free. I have also had time to think, and whilst I know I love and care for Anita, I'm not sure she feels the same way about me. It has dawned on me that she only wanted the money and

I was a tool to get it for her. I am a total fool, a rather nasty one. Have you arrested Simon yet?"

"No, but we know where he is."

"If you do, can I be kept away from him? I do not doubt he would try to silence me, given the chance."

"Yes we can arrange that. Did you ring him the day of, or after the murder?"

"No way, no, he said we were not to."

"What about the barbeque?"

"Oh yes, that was Simon too. He came and gave me a couple of bottles of wine and said we could have some fun with them. He suggested I gave them to certain members of the society, for a laugh. Like a fool, I did, I thought there was something like Viagra in them. He was planning all this then I think."

"Do you wish to apply for bail?"

"No, there is no point, Mr Farmer here has explained all that. I will be safer out of the way of Simon and that means in prison. I intend to plead guilty."

"Mr Farmer have you anything to add?"

"Not at this time. Tom and I had a long talk earlier, and he has made the decision to tell you this of his own free will."

"Alan, anything?"

"Just one thing, do you know where Simon got the idea for the axe?"

"He said he'd picked it up in Asia."

"Have you ever had anything to do with magic tricks?"

"No, but Anita has. A couple of times. I don't like it."

The interview terminated and when they had finished, they were met by Paul who told them that Anita had also admitted some of it, but said it was all Cantone's idea, and that she and Hobbs were set up by him. After a brief discussion, Saul directed both of them to be charged with conspiracy to murder as a holding charge. Saul said he was off to get some warrants and advised that Cantone should be regarded as a Category A prisoner.

Chapter Seven

Later that evening Saul was reading through Anita Jones confession.

'I first met Simon Hobbs or Dobbs as he was then, when I was a chorus girl at a nightclub in Birmingham. I was in a dreadful fix. I owed a lot of money, never mind what for, and my landlord wanted to put me on the game in payment of the rent. Simon needed to marry, to inherit some money. I have always known he liked both men and women, or more correctly lads and lasses. We did sleep together occasionally. Simon sorted the landlord out. Simon became more and more bizarre in his demands and we agreed to divorce. He paid me enough, and we went our separate ways. I did know I was pregnant by this time but thought if I told him he would have a hold on me, I had the child adopted, and said I didn't know who the father was.

I didn't meet Simon again for ages, by that time I was married to Ptolemy, and he wanted children, but I didn't. I never have. I never really loved Ptolemy either. I thought he had money, but I was wrong. Then Cyril started seeing me and promised me the earth. I knew he had money, lots of it. He was nasty, controlling, and wouldn't let me do what I wanted. He expected me to do housework and pander to his needs. He wouldn't let me out except to come to the operatic about which he was fanatical. I got very bored of him, very quickly. Then I started seeing Tom who was much more fun. Cyril had made me sign a prenuptial agreement before we married so if I left him or we divorced, I would get nothing, and he had a hell of a lot. I was trapped. Tom would have done anything for me.

Then my son Jason turned up. I sort of had to tell Simon when Jason demanded a DNA test. We all met at Tom's place. Simon was furious with me for not telling him. Of course Cyril knew nothing about it. Then Tom and Simon hatched this thing up between them; said it would scare Cyril into letting me go with enough money to be comfortable. It was, I think Tom's idea, but Simon knew all about it. I had to put the dummy axe in the normal place and with a handkerchief put the other one in the dressing room. Simon was going to swap them back. I did all that while the two of them watched me, to make sure I got it right. I don't know why they couldn't have done it. Then after 'Three Little Maids' I went down to the ladies' dressing room and then they told me Cyril was dead. I was ever so upset. The next day Tom told me Simon had set both of us up and we would be blamed. He said we needed to get out of the country before the police caught us. We had booked everything ages before, Tom said it was a precaution. I went to the airport all prepared but you lot were there waiting, as I now know. I thought we had got away with it.'

By the time Saul had re-read it and caught up on other paperwork it was about nine p.m. Alan rang and said that Hobbs had been detained in Rotherham, and Saul and he went down with a uniform escort to pick Hobbs up.

At Rotherham they were met by a CID officer who explained the circumstances of the arrest and handed over all property found when Hobbs had been arrested. Having completed all the custody records and paperwork and having put the property in their car, Hobbs was brought out from his cell.

"Oh, duckie, have you come to rescue me? There has been some dreadful mistake. They think I am involved in poor Cyril's murder. I just knew you two sweet peas would come to my rescue."

Alan informed him he was under arrest for murder and conspiracy to murder. Simon Hobbs' attitude changed immediately and the sly rather menacing look he gave Saul was rather unnerving. Simon spat at Saul, but missed and said, "Then you traitorous bitch, I am saying nothing."

Saul replied, "Good, I was not going to discuss it with you anyway, until the formal interview. This is

WPC Lancashire who will monitor you in the back of the van and I will be in the vehicle behind."

"You can't make me be supervised by a woman. Why can't you sit with me?"

The journey was uneventful, and Hobbs was booked into the cells at Saul's main station and as he and Alan were leaving the custody sergeant said, "Oh, sir, I thought you might like to know: those three boys who you arrested for robbery are back in custody, this time it was a pensioner they mugged. The poor lady, she is at Jimmy's with a fractured hip. She will, hopefully, be all right but as she is over eighty, we are worried. Apparently, they ran away from the care home."

"Thank you. How come they were not in a secure unit?"

"Some social worker vouched for them, said they were misunderstood. By her, no doubt. I have had them in before, you know."

"Yes, let's hope the lady recovers. Keep a close watch on Hobbs, he may try something."

"I will, sir. Do I let him have a phone call, if he asks?"

"To a solicitor, yes, but make sure you dial the number, and make sure it is a solicitor."

As they left Saul turned to Sandra Lancashire and said, "Thanks for that. Did I hear you are getting married soon?"

"Yes to Henry Birtwhistle, Billy's brother. We want you to come. Oh and we tried to find Diana Green but were told she was dead. Is that true?"

"I was told so, yes."

Saul dropped Alan off at his flat and drove home. Hercules greeted him enthusiastically with what remained of his slippers. The only ones up were Jake and Anna. When he went into the lounge, he could see Anna was upset. He hurried over and sat beside her and said, "Whatever is the matter?"

At this his wife burst into tears and grabbed a handful of tissues and tried to stop crying. Jake said, "It's her sister, Ruth. She rang about an hour ago. I don't know what she said, but Anna has been crying ever since, something about money. I'd just calmed her down. Saul, take over and I'll fix us a drink."

Saul, putting his arm around her, and grasping her hand said, "Now, Anna, tell me,"

"What we thought. She accused me of sucking up to Aunt Matilda, of stealing money from her! Saul, she said she only agreed to bring me up on the condition she was left the lot! She told me I was a grasping, ungrateful little traitor who was never going to see a penny of it. She said she is challenging the will and I am not getting any of it. Then she said you put me up to it, and that Stephen was as bad as you. Saul, it was a really spiteful, horrid tirade."

"My darling, you know none of that is true."

"I never sucked up to Aunt Matilda, just helped and visited when I could. Yes, we had her to stay after her hip operation, because Ruth wouldn't and said she didn't have the time."

Jake handed them both a drink and said, "The spiteful bitch! Are we talking much money?"

"Yes quite a lot. Ruth has been left the house, and contents, and Anna has been left the rest."

"Blimey, that is a lot, that house is worth a fortune. Is she not satisfied with that?"

Anna said, "I don't know. You're wrong, Saul, it was left to you and me together. A letter came from the solicitor's today. It's on the table there."

Saul fetched the letter, read it, and passed it to Jake. He then opened another envelope and said, "This is a letter from Matilda to me, personally. I will read it.

'My dear Saul,

I have just re-made my will, which you will, no doubt be told about. I have left most of my considerable fortune to you and Anna, jointly, for a specific reason. I will explain.

Ruth has always assumed she would be my sole beneficiary, although I always told her she would not. When their parents died, Ruth was old enough to look after Anna, and although I offered both of them a home

132

with me, Ruth refused it, and refused to let Anna come to me. I paid all their expenses from the time their parents died, more than willingly, and often Ruth would ask or demand more, saying it was to help Anna. I found out later that the monies I gave her were not used for that purpose at all.

When you were so badly injured, and Ruth behaved so badly towards you and your two sons, Stephen came to see me and told me all about it. I have always liked you; you are a good husband and father and I know you are a sound man with principles. I tackled Ruth about it later and she was most evasive. I never have liked being lied to and I didn't like the way she tried to manipulate her little sister. You rescued Anna from that. About a year ago, after I had my hip replaced, she suggested I went into a home for the elderly and it was ridiculous to live in this enormous house and pay for carers to come in. That was when you and Anna, kindly invited me to stay and nursed me back to health, for which I am profoundly grateful. She asked then if I would gift her the house, so she could live in it and I could find somewhere smaller, or better a retirement home. I then found out she wanted to turn my house, in which I have spent my whole life, into a refuge for lesbian women. Of that I strongly disapprove and told her no. When I was gone then she would have the house but with conditions attached. I saw a very nasty side to her then. To be honest she frightened me. I therefore changed my will, as I knew then she would try to trick or coerce or force Anna to give her more money. For this reason, I have left the remains of my wealth, which as you know is quite considerable, to you and your wife, jointly but I have placed a caveat on it. This is that the house I now live in and will leave for Ruth may only be used as a private residence, without multiple occupation, or it must be sold. You and Anna must not gift any monies left to you, to Ruth. Anna may well wish to give Ruth more, she is a kind person, but I believe you will be strong enough not to. Please make sure you, your children, family and all your grandchildren enjoy the money and put it to a good purpose. Ruth, if she does sell this house, which is very large, will be quite wealthy in her own right and so do not let her greed wear you or your family down. I have made sure Ruth will not be able to contest this will. If she does, then she will get only a small yearly income. She has already suggested that I am not of sound mind and should be sectioned.

I have left another sum to you personally for another purpose. I want you to do something for me. Sometime ago we discussed setting up a charity or trust fund to help young people who whilst not being classified as having problems may not be quite as sharp as they need to be to have a good life. I am not talking about bad children, but perhaps a family who could do well with a bit of help. I wonder if we could use some of the properties I own, to settle them in a good area. We spoke about this and all I ask is you set it up, and when you retire or even if you have time before, you become a trustee. I would also ask that with some of the money you find a young artist, under eighteen, to give a bursary to art school with.

You have made my niece very happy and I am gratefully yours,

Matilda, Agatha Sacree'.

Saul read the solicitor's accompanying letter and then said, "That explains a lot. Here read this. I will deal with Ruth and will do as Matilda requested."

"I think it might be a good idea, little brother, if I hang around here for a while. Just in case."

"Thank you, Jake, I would appreciate it."

Chapter Eight

Saul was first into the office in the morning. On his desk was a message from the ACC who told him it would be some days before the complaint against him could be resolved, as it was important that everything was correctly and thoroughly investigated. Together with Alan he later went and interviewed Hobbs. There was a solicitor present who Saul knew as a local duty solicitor who was regularly on call for the station. They put Cantone's version of events to Hobbs, who shrugged his shoulders and said, "Prove it"

Alan showed him a picture of one of the books from Hobbs' flat, that had illustrations of a similar axe device. Hobbs said, "That's not mine, it must be Charlie's."

Hobbs admitted that he had been married to Anita, and said, "She was a slag when I met her, all she ever wanted was money. I'm not even sure the child is mine. She had no right not to tell me if it was."

To every other thing they asked him his comment was either "no comment" or total silence.

Alan did most of the talking. During the interview Hobbs showed signs of being ill at ease and whenever Anita was mentioned a look of sheer hatred came over his face.

After the interview Saul said, "Looks like we will have to prove it, every bit of it. He is far too clever to admit anything. I wonder how a jury will assess him. By all means run it through with me and tell me what you need. I need next Saturday off, but otherwise I will help all I can. Just at the moment I am having a few family problems, but that aside, if you want to come over to mine for a drink or to chat, please do. How about this evening?"

"I rather hoped to go to a meeting this evening, at HQ. Caroline asked me to go with her. It is the Christian Police Association."

"No problem, I will be the one on call then. Tell me do you have much family?"

"None now. I was fostered most of my childhood. My mother never really wanted to know me. I was very lucky, my foster father was a brilliant barrister, a silk. He specialized in Offences against the Person."

"Not Alexis Withers, the author of several books. I've got them, even met him a couple of times. My word he was a fine man. I had heard he had passed away not long ago. So, what did you do for education?"

"I went to King's School Canterbury, then to university where I got a degree in modern languages, and then I tried the Immigration Service but didn't really like it, so I joined up."

"What did your dad think about that?"

"He approved, very much. I have a question for you, why are you being so nice to me? So kind. I know you do the best for your team, take an interest and all that, but it is as if I were a family member?"

"Because, Alan, for the first time I have met someone who I really understand, like and who I feel will one day take over from me. You are very bright, and principled. You even passed the vital test!"

"What test?"

"The one about having the right sense of humour. The cartoon you did showed me you have the kind of mind I understand. If you can take the mickey out of me then you can out of yourself. It is important."

"Why?"

"Because the man or woman who can laugh at themselves will never get so swollen headed as to push their brains out of their skull."

They had not been back in the Squad office for very long when Saul got a phone call from Jake. "Can you get home? Ruth is here, being very beastly to Anna, making her cry. I've tried putting her out once, but she is standing in the road, shouting the most offensive things. If I go out I will deck her at the least. I've managed to get the girls out of the way to next door and I'll take them back to school, but I'm not leaving until you get here. I won't leave Anna."

"Alan, I have to get home. A family emergency. Either my brother or I will probably end up hitting my sister-in-law who is being horrid to my wife."

"In which case I will come with you to act as a buffer. We'll take my car. I doubt a brawl would impress Complaints and Discipline at the moment. Paul, you're in charge."

Alan drove them back to Saul's home as fast as he could, and when they got there quite a crowd had assembled, including the paper boy, tradesmen, and several neighbours They could hear the three dogs barking inside the house, and Jake was standing in the front doorway, barring any access. Ruth, looking ridiculous, was hitting the door and Jake with the remains of a plant pot. There was soil and broken vegetation all over the drive and porch, and Ruth was screaming abuse, most of which was a variation of "Traitor, Jew Thieving Judas, a bloody house full of Jews, isn't one enough!"

Alan called for backup on his police radio and rushed to be with Saul as he got out of the car.

"Holy Moses, she's flipped, I think she is having a breakdown."

Alan shouted to Jake, "Get him inside, then come and help me."

Saul ran up the path, neatly side-stepping Ruth who by this time was wielding a piece of trellis torn from the front of the house. Ruth lunged at him and swiftly ducking under Jake's arm, Saul got into the house and through to the kitchen, where he was relieved to find Anna and their neighbor, Josie, comforting her. As he got to them the sound of smashing glass echoed through the house from the lounge. Anna stood up, but Saul said, "No let the others deal with it. Thanks for being here, Josie. I am grateful."

"Look, Saul, I will put the kettle on, and I have rung Salim and he is already taking the girls back to their school. Fortunately, they were at ours when she turned up. Salim fetched their bags and they were long gone before she really kicked off. Jake told me to ring 999 so I did. She has been saying and screaming the most foul things mainly about you but also to Anna, and then when your brother wouldn't let her in, about me. She got really violent and hit him over the head with a flower pot, a large one. All he did was keep her out. He didn't hit her back. I would have done!"

"How much did the girls see?"

"Not much. They were with my two, Yasmin and Selina, and I told them Ruth was ill and to stay out of it. Here, tea. Saul, sit down, you are not going to go out there and get involved. Anna needs you here with her. What has brought this on?"

"Anna has been left some money by an aunt that Ruth thinks should have come to her. She has never liked me and was against our marriage, Ruth I mean not the aunt."

"Yes, I think I understand. The trouble like mixed marriages such as we have, it gives some people a reason for hating because they don't approve. My parents did not like my marrying Salim and when I introduced them to you, they asked about you. I think my mother knew you were Jewish."

"Yes, and we couldn't ask for better neighbours. It sounds like the troops have arrived. I wonder how long Ruth can keep the screeching up?"

"Really, Saul! I know she can do it for ages. You know this isn't the first time she has flipped like this. I never told you, but she did it before our wedding. She has always hated you, and apparently your religion."

"She has enjoyed our hospitality often enough!"

"I think she always hoped I would leave you."

"When did you last see Ruth, Anna?"

"A fortnight ago, she met me in town for a coffee. She was telling me all about her new companion, lover, and what they were going to do with Matilda's money. She suggested I leave you and was most put out when I said I wasn't going to. That was the last time I saw her, after Matilda's funeral."

"No, Anna, Saul, she was here two days ago. I saw her in a car up the road. With another woman. I thought they must be coming to visit but I never saw them get out of the car. I think you had other guests then."

"Interesting. Anna, did she say what this new girlfriend of hers did for a living? Or mention a name?"

"Yes Yvonne, something, it was a double-barrelled name. She said she was a senior social worker."

"It wasn't Salter-Hicks by any chance was it?"

"Yes, why do you know her?"

"We have met, yes. It's gone awfully quiet out there, maybe I should check all is OK. Oh, that sounds like Jake coming in. I'd better go and see the damage."

Alan came in with Jake and two uniformed PCs. He said, "Sit down, and let me get a medic to check that cut on your head. It's all right, Saul. I had to nick her, and she has gone. I did try to reason with her."

Jake chuckled. "Yes, you were very restrained especially when she kicked you."

"What was the screeching about?"

"I touched her, to hold her arm when I was arresting her. She was trying to hit me. She only stopped screeching when a WPC took over. I am sorry, Anna, but I don't like your sister very much."

"Nor do I, Alan. Are you hurt?"

"I'll have a hefty bruise but nothing worse, it is Jake who is bleeding. I'll call a medic."

"Let me have a look at him first. I am sorry I don't know your name but I live next door and I am a nurse. I'll fix him up or take him to a doctor if needed. I am Josinda Khan. Jake, sit still. No, I think it just needs a bandage. I'll check it in a while when the blood has clotted. Now, you, young detective policeman, let me see that bruise."

Alan, knowing when to gracefully give in sat down and said, "Thank you, Saul, I am sorry about the window. She picked up that hydrangea in a pot and chucked it. I am fit but I struggled to lift it just now. Before I head down to the local nick, can I have a word? These uniform officers are taking statements from everyone: your neighbours, the fish man, the paper boy, the plumber from down the road, a passing cyclist and the gardener from no 42. Would you give one, Mrs Khan?"

"Yes, dear, and my husband will as soon as he gets back. He rang just now to say he would not be long. Keep still and I'll put a cold compress on that; it is a nasty bruise. Not from a kick, I don't think. It was a punch and they were wearing a ring because it has cut you slightly. I'll just put some antiseptic on."

Alan, wincing while Josie was examining him, said, "I have a photographer coming and Scenes of Crime. Please don't clear up until they have been."

Saul went out into the front garden and surveyed the damage. He saw his front door was on its hinges and splintered by the glass panel that had been in it and was now in pieces all over the drive. One of his lounge windows was smashed. There were several broken flower pots and the trellis was missing and there was earth and dirt everywhere. He looked down at a small broken glass bottle and noticed a liquid bubbling and fizzing beside it. He called an officer over and said, "Do we know what this is?"

"No, sir, the large gentleman said not to touch it, he thought it was acid."

Jake arrived with a bandage around his head, "Yes, when she arrived, she demanded to see you. Not Anna. She said she knew you were at home as you had been suspended. She said, and I quote, 'Anna won't want him when he's worn that'. She threw it at me but missed. I think it is acid."

Alan joined them minutes later, and Saul said, "Alan, thank you. Look I need to tell you. You know the woman who complained about me?"

"Not personally but you said she was a social worker."

"Yvonne Salter-Hicks, and she is Ruth's now new live in lover. I think I need to tell the ACC from Complaints and Discipline about this. I'd better ring him."

"No, Saul, I will. Better coming from me. Keep out of it. I must go. See you soon. All your neighbours have offered to come and help and are waiting for the SOCO to finish. I am not even going to ask if you wish to press charges because I am."

Saul was more shaken than he cared to admit. He rang the school, spoke to and reassured his daughters, and thanked all his neighbours. Jake offered to repair the door and to make a new one to fit later. Jake, having finally sat down with a brandy, said, "I like Alan, he is sound. He reminds me a bit of you as a younger man, in the way he took charge. Quite unflappable he was. Is it OK if I stay on for a few days?"

"Thanks, little brother, I'd be very grateful. I see you found the better brandy, pour me another, will you?"

Alan was kept very busy for most of the evening. Ruth, after causing havoc in the cell block, was committed and taken to a mental hospital where she was detained for twenty-eight days. He rang the Assistant Chief Constable and updated him of the situation. He put the file together with the assistance of a couple of the squad and the typist, Janice. He got to his meeting just in time. He went back to the office about ten and the phone was ringing. "Murder Squad, DI Withers speaking."

"Is Saul there?"

"No, not at the moment, who is calling?"

"Tell him Diana rang. I'll speak to him tomorrow. Could you tell him to look up his Stevenson? He'll understand. I rang his home but someone I didn't know answered, a woman."

"Yes, his neighbours are there. I am his deputy. Can I help?"

"No, sorry. He'll understand."

"Fine. I'll do that. Diana who?"

"Just Diana. What happened to Celia?"

"She got promoted."

"Good, I expect we will meet soon. Don't forget to tell him, please."

"I won't."

Once Alan was back at his flat and had thought about it, he rang Saul and passed on the message. Saul said, "Oh that is wonderful, yes I understand. It will cheer Anna up no end. I can't explain. I'll see you first thing. Can you come for breakfast and give me a lift into work?"

Chapter Nine

Hobbs was remanded in custody and sent to a different prison to that in which Cantone was being held. The whole team worked very hard the whole of the morning, and after everyone had returned from lunch Saul called a meeting. They gathered their notes, and their coffees and a large box of chocolates and Saul said, "Thank you, everyone, for what you are doing. I know all of you have worked long hours and very hard. Oh, all right, is there a coffee crème left? Whose birthday is it?"

"No one's that we know of we just thought it might cheer us up."

"Thank you, Tarik. Now, Paul, did you see your magician?"

"Yes, he was very helpful and put me in touch with the committee of the Magic Circle, who have been very helpful indeed, and their evidence will be invaluable. What I didn't know was that they keep a sort of index of all this kind of trick, and a record of who knows or uses them, and one of them was Simon Dobbs as they knew him. They also have Anita down as being his stage partner, so she would also have known how it worked.

They showed me too and it is quite ingenious. I videoed that."

"Fantastic, I know you have all worked long hours and gone without your rest days, so anyone who wants, please take some days off. Obviously, I would prefer them to be staggered. I will happily come and do a day in the office so Fred or Nita can have a couple of days."

Fred said, "No, guv, I'm quite happy to come in. My wife is away and I'd only get bored at home, and if I am there my neighbour will insist on my going to them for a meal, and it would take hours and I don't really like spicy food."

"I need to finish the file I had on that mugging I took on a couple of months ago, and I can do that and help in the office."

"Right, Julia, thank you. Now if you can sort it, I will see you all in three days' time."

"That would be the seventeenth, sir. You will be here?"

"Yes, Fred, why?"

"No reason, we'll see you then, sir."

Saul wondered why they had made a point of the date but a bit later in the afternoon Alan put some paperwork on his desk and together they went through the file. Then Saul said, "You too, Alan, have a break if you want one. I am off to see someone, social, to get a bit of advice."

"Your old boss? Can I come I'd love to meet him? I've heard about him."

"In which case we'd better stop off at an off licence on the way."

Duffy, as usual was expostulating about something on the television, a police programme. When he saw Saul enter the room he smiled and said, "Hello, lad, come to comfort an old man? Who is this whippersnapper with you?"

"This is my new DI, Duffy. I think you'll like him. I do, and I can trust him."

"That will do for me then. Something's troubling you, lad, I can tell. Sit down and tell me all about it."

"Yes, I do need your advice. Alan here knows about it."

"In which case you push off and get me and you two some tea and some flapjacks and let him tell me. He looks capable of coherent speech."

Alan told Duffy everything he knew, both about the case and about the complaint against Saul and about Ruth. He also told Duffy what Jake had confided to him in an early morning phone call. Duffy sat back and listened carefully and took some notes on a pad.

When Alan had finished Duffy looked at him. "You have a good head on your shoulders and you are so like Saul at your age it is almost uncanny. I see why he likes you. Yes, he does seem to have a bit of a problem. He is obviously beating himself up inside about it but won't let anyone else shoulder some of the stress. He will to me, which is why he came. My body may be failing but my mind is not. Yes, I remember Ruth Hughes, only too well. Nasty spiteful bitch. She tried to make a lot of trouble for Saul years ago. She actually came to see me and told me a cock and bull story about him mistreating Anna, or as she insisted on calling her sister, Dianna, which she stopped using years ago. Ruth told me he was cheating on her, bleeding her of money and that he was in fact, corrupt and stealing from the force. She asked me to get him out of the job, or at least moved away. I listened and made some enquiries and established that it was all a malicious fantasy of hers and she was lying about everything.

"I went to see Anna without telling Saul and offered help, if she needed it. She laughed and explained that none of it was true and she was deeply in love with a wonderful man. At this time she was pregnant with their youngest. Ruth had considered that he had mistreated her by getting her pregnant. Another nasty allegation Ruth made was that Saul had tried to rape her, and when I pressed her for details, I was able to prove that not only had nothing like that happened, Saul was down south, on some course and had a solid alibi for the time. I know because I was with him on the evening she alleged it had happened. I had gone down to discuss a case with him.

It was in Hampshire, at Bramshill. I made enquiries about Ruth then. What I found out was interesting. As a child she had been apt to make ridiculous stories up, mainly about her father. When she was very little, she had several times tried to hurt or kill Anna. It was assumed it was jealousy. I don't think Anna ever knew that. I spoke to their family doctor about it and he said she was a compulsive liar. He's still alive, lives in Bradford. I'll give you his address and I think you or this ACC should talk to him. He also told me he wondered if Ruth had not, in fact, killed her parents. There was no evidence of course but I too wondered. Then she took up rearing Anna and seemed to change for the better. I still have a file I kept. I'll tell you how to get it."

"Does Saul know any of this?"

"No, Anna and I decided it wouldn't help him. I know that Ruth went off to a boarding school and did very well and eventually became a teacher and seemed to be all right. I remember Anna telling me that whenever their parents tried to discipline Ruth there would be a nasty accident shortly afterwards. When Ruth came back from teacher training, she was apparently a devoted and caring sister to Anna. Now Anna told none of this to Saul because she wanted to leave it behind and as Saul is very sensitive, she didn't want him to know. Ah, tea and double flapjacks, well done, I'm parched and, Saul, you clever cub, doughnuts. Well done!"

When Alan presented Duffy with a bottle of Glenlivet as well as the one Saul had presented, Duffy chuckled and said, "I do like you. You can come again. You will, won't you? You don't need to bring this boring old fart with you. I knew your father I think, clever chap. Excellent brain. Is he still alive?"

"No, he died three years ago."

"I'm sorry. You don't look like him!"

"He was my foster father. I will come and see you."

"Good, now push off and let me talk to Saul alone. See you soon, Mowgli."

"Certainly, Akela, just be gentle with Bagheera here, won't you?"

As Alan left, Duffy said,

"Not only bright, but caring and well-read too. He'll take over from you, I expect. Good education, excellent manners. Good choice for a second in command. I approve. I couldn't stand your last one."

"She was all right, he's in a different class."

"Yes. Well now, listen, Baggypants, I need to tell you rather a lot. You won't like it much, and you are not to fall out with that lovely wife of yours over it."

"Baggypants! Really, Duffy."

"Yes, you've got too thin of late. Not ill, are you?"

"No, I'm fine. I've taken up swimming, for the leg."

When Saul left some two hours later, he was stunned. Duffy had told him everything and had explained a lot. Saul had never pushed his wife over things she had been through in her childhood. That she had been troubled he had known, but she had always said that being with him had taken the troubles away. What Duffy had told him had angered him, but Duffy had calmed him down. Saul very much wanted to go home and be with Anna. He also wanted to tell Jake. He called in at the office, to check his messages, and found one from the ACC. He rang him. "Sir, you wanted to talk to me?"

"I spoke to Withers, and your chief, and I have just had a call from Duff. I think I may have done you an injustice. Don't fret about it. I'll be in to see you next week. Whatever you do, do not try to contact this Salter-Hicks woman."

"I won't, thank you, sir."

No sooner had he put the phone down than it rang again. "Catchpole."

"Saul, it's Diana. Did you get my message?"

"Yes, can you come and stay?"

"Only if I am not in the way. You couldn't pick me up at Leeds station?"

"Now? Yes, where will you be?"

"Wait in WHSmith. The big one, I'll find you."

When Saul got to the station it was very crowded. Nowhere could he see Diana. He went to WHSmith and was looking at some paperbacks when a smart blonde woman came and stood beside him, wearing what looked like Gucci shoes and a very elegant trouser suit.

"Thanks for coming, you did say once, so I took you up on your offer. Can I buy you a coffee?"

"You look stunning. Is this the real you?"

"No, I am much more casual. I am sorry, I owe you an apology, and an explanation. I wouldn't be offended if you told me to go to hell."

"Don't be ridiculous. Come let's get that coffee."

They sat at a table and over a coffee he said, "We have been hoping you would come. I must tell you we have a house guest, my brother Jake. He thinks he knew you. Out east. Not under his name. Is that a problem for you?"

"Big man, long red hair, ridiculous beard, swears like a trooper and looks a bit like you?"

"That's him."

"No, it's not a problem. I really liked him; we worked together. When I met you, you reminded me of him?"

"You are sure. I can get him to go home?"

"No need, I would very much like to meet him again. He is no danger to me at all. What's worrying you?"

"Family and work problems. I could do with your advice. Have you any luggage?"

"Yes, a bit, in the left luggage."

"How do you change your appearance like that?"

"Easily. I have very ordinary features. Nothing outstanding or memorable. It is amazing what a bit of make-up and the right clothes will do. I just don't have a memorable face. Look, I don't want to cause you any upset or further problems. I could come another time."

"Why change the habits of a lifetime? No, I think your being here could help a lot. I hope you can stay a while?"

"My time is my own now. I've finally retired. I was going to ask for your advice too, about something but it will wait."

"What do I call you?"

"Diana will do."

"Is it really your name?"

"It is one of them. It is now. My name is officially Diana White, unless I want to change it."

"Not Boddington?"

"Not anymore."

"Come on, my car's out the front."

When they reached the car, and loaded it, he said, "Is that all your luggage?"

"Yes my worldly possessions. Not much for a lifetime really, is it?"

When they arrived at the house, the garden was once more immaculate, the front door was repaired, and Jake came out to greet them. He stared at Diana and said, "You don't know how happy I am to see you. I hardly know you. Saul, you clever dog! Anna will be thrilled."

Hercules and the two Labradors burst past Jake onto the drive and rushed towards Diana. Jake went to stop them, but Saul said, "No, watch, see what happens."

The dogs were in ecstasy. They submitted immediately and rolled over begging for a tummy rub, which they got, and Diana said, "Inside all of you. Behave yourselves and yes, I am pleased to see you. What is this monster called?"

"Hercules, and I have NEVER seen him fawn over anyone like that before!"

"Dogs and I get on."

Saul said, "Yes, I went to check that Drift was happy. She is, very, will you get her back?"

"No, she will be happier where she is; Janet will look after her. She deserved retirement too. Thanks for telling me that."

They went inside with the dogs demurely walking at Diana's heels. Anna coming from the kitchen gave a cry of delight and rushed forward and embraced Di. "You came, how wonderful. Thank God! I'll make up Stephen's room for you."

"No, I'll do it. Thanks Saul. That bag there, and that one, are both for you and Anna, so is the box. I am sure you will appreciate the box, Jake."

In the box was a crate of wine. "Only the best, eh, Di. Thanks, what is in the bags, Anna?"

"This crystal it is beautiful like the other set you sent us, but the design is different. Oh, look some orchids too. We have a few now."

Saul looked at the orchid plants and said, "Is this a new one? I've not heard of it before. That one I know is called Diana. It was exhibited at Chelsea this year, but I couldn't buy one. I was told it was not for sale."

"Yes, well let's just say I know the woman who grew them. The other one will be at Chelsea this year; it is called Moonshine. Now where are the sheets or do I unpack my own? I get the feeling you and Saul need to talk. We can do it, can we not, Jake, and then we can walk the dogs for you? Jake, you can fill me in with what is going on. Who spilled acid on the drive recently?"

Saul and Anna sat in the lounge and were soon talking. Before long they heard Jake and Di go out with the dogs. By eleven they were beginning to wonder where they were and then Saul looked out of the front window, and said, "That's them! I suspect they have had a drink or two, Jake is weaving. The dogs look absolutely shattered, and they are all of them drenched."

While Jake took the dogs through to the utility room and dried them off, Saul handed a glass of wine to Di. "Thank you, but I'll only have the one, and I think Jake may have had a couple too many already. I'm sorry about the dogs. We passed a park on the way back and the lake was just too inviting. We'll talk in the morning unless you are working."

"No, I've the day off."

Jake grinned foolishly as he popped in to say goodnight. "You two OK? Good I'm off to sleep it off. She is the only woman I have ever met that could drink me under the table. I'll have to try another way to seduce her. Goodnight!"

When Saul and Anna came down the next morning Di had cleaned the utility room, cooked breakfast and walked the dogs. Jake came down looking like a large bear in his pyjamas and grunted before retreating back upstairs with a large coffee.

Anna said, "Di thanks. I'm sorry we had to talk last night."

"I understand. Jake explained a bit. If you need us out the way so you can talk some more, I am sure I can lead him astray today. He wants to show me his farm."

"No, I want to talk to you, so does Saul."

"Good I want to talk to you as well."

They adjourned a bit later when Jake had finally come down to the lounge. They talked for some time about the situation, and Di, returning with even more coffee said, "Right, I can't help you with Hobbs, but I can with Ruth. I know just how to do it. Then I will tell Alan. Which hospital is she in?"

"The Canterbury Institute. Just what are you proposing to do. I thought you said you had retired?"

"From one organization yes. This will be for fun. I read the local paper at the station yesterday. They are advertising for cleaners. I will apply tomorrow."

"I can't let you do that!"

"You can't stop me. Listen I love you two big time, and you both know it. I know you were upset when you thought I was dead. I hated having to deceive you; it was necessary. I know you tried to find me, the pair of you. You went for a break down to Somerset. Stayed at the George Hotel in Cheddar and went for several walks in Ebbor Gorge. It isn't that large a place, so you had to be looking for something. You were discreet, never asked for Georgina Boddington, but I know you hate caves, Saul. You went round the two show caves in Cheddar Gorge. You asked the lady at the ticket office how to get to Ebbor Gorge, said you'd heard it was pretty."

"How the hell did you know that?

"She said, yes but Burrington was more scenic, and you could do Ebbor in half a day. She then suggested the paper mill at Wookey Hole. You went the next day. You bought some presents at Cheddar, and some sweets;

I think the bill came to £17.03. Did you look at your receipt?"

"No, I don't think so."

"If you had you would have seen that the person serving you was called Diana."

"That was you?"

"Yes. I was very pleased to see you, and knew you cared. I couldn't reveal myself, not then. You looked me in the face, thanked me for my help and smiled."

"But that woman was at least sixty, more."

"I have told you before, I can be one of many people. How on earth did you find me at Tunbridge Wells?"

"That was pure chance. I was orchid hunting. I never knew it was you until you looked up. It shook me rigid, and I want to know, how did you get that note into my locked car?"

"It shook me up too. I was on a job. Getting into your car was easy. You had left the sun roof slightly open. I had time to write the note and put it in with a pair of long handled pruning shears. Then I hid and heard your reply. When you got back to work you did a check on all four cars in the car park there."

"I hope I didn't put you in danger?"

"No, you were not looking for a Priscilla Stanton."

"Why did you have to die?"

"I nearly did die. We had a leak, at quite a high level. Consequently, I have been on quite a few hit lists for some time. I started another job down in Cornwall, but they caught up with me there. If it hadn't been for a good landlady I would have died. She found me just in time. I 'died' at the hospital there and my body was taken away from their mortuary, by an undertaker. It took a long time to recover. I became someone else. Since then we have dealt with the leak and although I have now returned, I've sort of been pensioned off."

"Until the next time they need you."

"Yes, but I will have the choice, and I doubt I will. I was hoping to settle down and have some fun. I was worried I might meet Janet, I think I need to tell her."

"I can do that for you, she will want to give your dog back."

"No, but if I can meet her and explain…"

"You said you wanted some advice?"

"Yes, I need to find somewhere to settle, a medium size farm, where I can keep sheep, a horse and a few ducks and chickens and some pigs and cows. It is what I have always wanted."

"I can help you there, Di, come and live with me on my farm."

"Jake, really, but I would seek your advice. Do you know of any farms coming up for sale?"

"Depends on how big your budget is. I don't suppose you would marry me, would you?"

"I told you last night when you asked me then, that I'd think about it. I don't know you well enough yet. I do know you have a hell of a reputation with women. Just how many children have you got?"

"Ten or so that I know of. I see I shall have to court you properly, if you'll let me?"

"I expect I might quite enjoy that. Let's see how it goes. I am a demanding woman! If you are serious, the first thing you do is get a proper haircut, and shave off that ridiculous beard."

Saul and Anna had been sitting listening to this conversation, fascinated. They were laughing heartily, and Saul had to go and get a glass of water to stop his hiccups. He said, "Di, I think you got him there. He'll never shave that beard off; it is almost a religion with him."

"So he told me when we first met years ago. If he can make demands, then so can I."

"You really don't like it, do you?"

"Not much. I could never even consider an attachment to a man with a beard like that. Now, what shall I cook for lunch?"

After lunch they were having coffee in the lounge when two visitors arrived in quick succession. The first was Stephen who brought with him a parcel which he gave to Anna and she put away. He asked to talk to his father and they went into the study. Then Alan arrived and looked at Jake. "How are you, today, how's the head?"

"I've a bit of a headache, but not from being hit; I had way too much to drink last night." Jake was grinning and went and sat down.

Alan turned to Anna and asked after her. She said, "Much better thank you. Saul's busy right now but can I introduce you to Diana. This is Alan Withers."

They shook hands and Diana said, "Hello we spoke on the phone. I am Diana White, a family friend. Nice to meet you."

"Likewise, so you are the huntress coming home from the hill? I too looked up my Stevenson. I trust the Requiem is not applicable. Did they tell you what happened yesterday?"

"Yes, I need to talk to you about something. Why don't you help me get some tea?"

The two of them headed toward the kitchen and Anna looked at Jake and said, "Jake what are you playing at? You are not to hurt Diana, do you understand? Don't make out you want marriage. It isn't fair to joke like that."

"Who said anything about joking? I mean it. I will marry that woman, but maybe I was rushing it a bit. As

I said, I'll have to court her. Do you know what music she likes?"

"Yes, as a matter of fact I do. She told me once. Operas, classical, folk and she did mention Gregorian chant. I think she might be very musical."

"I see, right where is the local rag, I need to see what concerts are on. I know she likes fine food, and art."

"Are you serious?"

"Yes, I have never been more so in my life!"

"Don't ride roughshod over her emotions."

"Me? I couldn't make her do anything. She is an incredible person. I have never met her match. You are wonderful, but she is fantastic."

"Flattery, Jake? Now, was there any chance of you mending things in the conservatory?"

"She and I are going to do it this evening, while Saul takes you out for a meal."

"Does Saul know this?"

"Not yet, but he will. I will make Diana happy, believe me. Now, what does Stephen want? I think Saul has enough on his plate right now."

"I think he has just come to give support."

"Yes both your boys are fine young men. How do you feel about Ruth now?"

"I think I have always known something was wrong; when I was little, I was terrified of her. Then she changed and was very kind. She managed to put off my first two serious boyfriends, and tried it with Saul as well, but I knew he was the one for me. She tried to stop the wedding, and even after we had the kids, she tried to turn the girls against me. I do remember, just after Dad died, I defied her over something. I think it was my options at school, and she hit me several times. I have finally seen what she is like. I don't need her now, I need my real family. That love me."

Di and Alan came in with a tea tray, and Stephen and Saul came in and they all sat down. After tea Alan and Saul went to the study and had a brief chat and Alan updated Saul. As Alan went out into the hall to leave, Saul said, "Do you want to stay for supper?"

Jake joined them and said, "Another time, because you, Saul, are taking Anna out for a meal this evening."

"Am I? Oh, I see, what exactly are you planning, bro?"

"Furniture repairs."

"Jake, don't push Di please. Give her time?"

***

At breakfast the next morning, Jake announced he was going into town, and hitched a lift with Saul. Anna looked at Di. "Shopping?"

"Good idea, I need a few things, like a car, for starters. I also need to get a birthday present for Saul. It is tomorrow, isn't it?"

"Yes, and I know what he would like, a new paint box. Jake is getting him slippers to replace the ones Hercules ate. Look, Di, we need to talk."

"Have I offended you in some way, if so, I apologize."

"No don't be daft. I need to talk about Jake. I don't want either of you hurt. He is deeply in love with you."

"Well I've known that for a long time. I know he's not joking. I just need a bit of time to adapt and to make him feel he has earned my love. I am not going to fold at the first hurdle!"

"You are saying you could consider it?"

"Very much so. I hope this doesn't upset you and Saul?"

"You don't mind about his children, all his affairs?"

"Not if he doesn't. He won't have any more, not if he wants to stop with me."

"I should imagine you will have dreadful rows."

"Probably but under that bear like exterior he is a soft teddy bear. We will have a lot of fun making up."

"Good luck, now you said a car, to start with. What had you in mind?"

"Can we go to the Land Rover dealers? And then we will hit the shops, big style."

166

They spent a wonderful day shopping and decided not to tell Saul until later. Jake took the dogs for a long walk at lunch time and finished mending furniture, and at tea time everyone came home.

Saul looked at Jake and started laughing.

"It's not that funny, Saul."

"It's hilarious, I must say it takes about ten years off you. Are they new clothes too?"

"Yes, if you must know, they are. I need to smarten up. I've ordered some suits from our brother as well."

When he greeted the ladies, Anna's jaw dropped in astonishment. Jake had not only had a haircut, he was clean shaven, and looked very respectable.

Diana said, "That's better, about time too. New clothes as well. Yes, you can take me to a concert tonight. Are you two coming?"

Saul, still trying not to laugh said, "No, you two love birds go, we will enjoy a quiet evening in."

Chapter Ten

When Saul got into the office the next morning, he was very early but was amazed that all the team were in already. There was a coffee waiting on his desk and everyone was grinning at him. He became very suspicious and said to Nita, "Right what is going on?"

"Nothing, sir, nothing at all. That ACC is coming in at eleven to see you, and the coroner wants a word, and if you can sign some of the paperwork off, I can get it out."

Saul looked up and instantly everyone looked away and began to busy.

"Well, something's going on."

"Really, sir?"

He rang, and then visited the coroner, and then called in to see Sgt Pepper. "Lonely, how is the case with these three lads going? I heard they had been in again. Do we know how the old lady is?"

"She is doing all right. We've cleared up a lot of robberies. The case conference is this afternoon. They have appointed a different social worker, not sure why. I gather the original one has been suspended. I wasn't told why."

"Do you need me for anything?"

"No thanks, sir, I will keep you posted. That ACC is coming to see me at twelve. I spoke to him a couple of days ago, told him the score. He wants a copy of the file. I'll give it to him when he comes in. How's your murder coming on?"

"Quite well. The coroner has released the body, and I have found a relative, and the funeral will be next week. Look, would it inconvenience your case or you if I contacted young Jonathan's mother?"

"Not at all, why?"

"I wanted to ask her about something, nothing to do with the case. I got the impression she hated living on that estate. I may be able to offer her another place to live. I wondered where she worked."

"At the chocolate factory. She has to travel quite a way."

"Fine thanks. I have mountains of paperwork to clear, so I must be off."

Back at his office Saul was making good progress. The ACC came to see him and discussed the whole matter about the bus. Wally was there as well and when they had finished discussing the matter Saul and Wally accompanied the visitor to his car outside in the yard. They returned to the squad room where the whole squad was waiting and on the large table was an enormous birthday cake, with the appropriate number of lit candles, and there were balloons everywhere. To many cries of "Happy Birthday" Saul looked around.

Wally said, "I didn't know. Many happy returns Saul. Your squad think a lot of you, it would seem."

Saul seldom blushed and on this occasion he did. "So that is what was up. Thank you, all of you. I suppose this means you will all join me for a drink at the bar in the social club after work? It is a very large cake. Who made it?"

"Several of us combined, sir. We know you are going through a tough time at the moment and hoped it would cheer you a bit."

"Well thank you, Julia, and all of you. It has. Now if you were thinking of singing 'Happy Birthday' I shall cry with embarrassment. What is this?"

Several parcels had appeared on the table. He opened a large flat one and found a brilliant cartoon framed and he laughed at it. "It is wonderful, who did it?"

Tarik said, "I am afraid that's me, sir. Look we heard you might be in need of some garden things, so we got you these plant pots and stuff."

Saul shot a look at Alan who winked at him and smiled.

"Well both my wife and I thank you. I would have had to get some, yes. Now work calls."

"Not until you have cut the cake, sir. We all want a bit."

At this point the chief constable walked in, and everyone jumped to their feet. Saul, with a large knife in his hand, looked faintly embarrassed.

"At ease, everyone. Saul, cut the cake and I will have a slice please. I just came to assure you I am fine with this. I knew what they planned and gave my consent. They cleared it with me days ago."

As the day progressed a constant stream of visitors came to see Saul and he caught up with colleagues, old friends, the cleaning staff, the warehouse man, the typists and the secretarial and civilian staff. Fred Dunlop came in and gave him yet more post.

"Fred, I am a bit taken aback. Why so much fuss, it is just a birthday? I am very flattered of course, but why this year?"

"I'll tell you why, sir, personally you have given me a chance to contribute something, until I get my pension. With MS I thought I would be out early. Nita, she thought she was going to have to be out on a medical after that accident. You are good to all of us and we appreciate it."

"What even, what was it, the gimlet eyes and the heavy frown?"

"Even that. You may get worried, hardly surprising but you are always fair with it. No one wants to cross you. But you stick up for us, and helped us all, in your quiet way. Take Geoff, he's going to be all right. You helped, young Andrew last year when his lad had that accident. Julia when her mother died. Celia when she mucked up. You could have made life hell for her, but you didn't."

"All right, enough! I like to repay loyalty with loyalty. It works both ways. Fred, how are you, physically I mean?"

"At the moment in remission. I know it won't last. I can do most things. I want to stay on as long as I can, and it looks like I will be able to stay for a full pension now."

Having bought everyone a drink at the bar, Saul was about to leave the social club when he spotted Anna, Jake and Diana come in. He resigned himself to a long haul. The party swelled as officers and friends he had known for many years joined in. Then he found Alan and said, "How am I going to get home? I'm over the limit now."

"All fixed, sir. I am taking you and your family home. I will pick you up in the morning. Don't try to pick up the tab at the bar, it's already taken care of."

"Who by?"

"Your brother. Oh good, the band's arrived. This has been planned for weeks, long before I arrived."

"I'm very flattered. You know I shall get my revenge?"

"Probably."

Saul enjoyed the rest of the evening, very much.

Over the next week Saul, Alan, Julia and Paul worked hard with the team gathering evidence and making enquiries. Forensic results came back and were very informative.

At home Saul and Anna saw little of Jake and Di, who would disappear with the dogs and come in, often fairly late, and when asked where they had been would say, "Out and about." As house guests they were no problem and even kept the house clean and tidy as well as preparing a variety of delicious meals.

Ruth had been detained in the hospital under a twenty-eight-day order. The next weekend Saul's two daughters came home from their boarding school and went with Jake and Di for a day on his farm. They came back filthy and having had a wonderful time.

Saul was sitting in his study when Di came in. "Something on your mind?"

"Yes, there is. I owe you and Anna an apology. I've rather neglected you, and treated the place a bit like a hotel. I'm sorry, I didn't mean to be so rude."

"You've done nothing of the sort. Hotel guests do not do the garden, mend the car, walk the dogs, clean the house and cook fantastic meals. We appreciate the time you have given us to talk things through."

"That was the least we could do, but it is time I moved on, got out of your hair."

"I hope not. You are welcome to stay for as long as you want. Anna said as much to me yesterday. Please don't go."

"I wasn't thinking of going far. I need my own base. I've put in an offer for the farm up the road from Jake's place. I think they will accept, and I should know in a couple of weeks. Oh, I was working at that hospital where Ruth is, only temporary like, and part time. I found out quite a lot and I have told Alan. I think it might help. I think I might be around your family for a long time. Do you mind?"

"No, I'm delighted. I have never seen Jake so happy, so civilized. He cares deeply for you."

"Yes, and I for him. Every day he has asked me to marry him."

"And?"

"I am going to say yes, very soon. I am convinced now, that he means it."

"Does he know what you are going to say?"

"I think so. Saul, I need you to do something for me. I know you are frantically busy, but it needs to be soon, and it has to be you."

"What? No hang on, you need me to see Janet, tell her."

"Yes please. Can you explain without going into detail what the score is, and assure her I do not want Drift back? I need to apologize to her."

"Actually, I think she might already have a clue, but I will go and see her tomorrow and explain, then you can meet up."

"Thank you. I owe you."

"Yes but I want something in return."

"Anything, if I can."

"I want you and Anna and Jake to help me run this charity with the families that need that kind of help. You might be able to find such families or kids."

"Good idea."

The next day Saul drove up to Janet's farm. He knocked on the door and Janet shouted from within, "Come in, whoever you are, mind the puppies!"

Saul stepped over a litter of collie pups and saw Drift rush back to guard them. Janet came through the door into the kitchen and said, "Mr Catchpole, come in. No trouble, I hope, as you see my hands are full. The kettle is on the hob there. Put it on will you?"

Saul spotted some mugs hanging on some hooks under the dresser top. He also saw a framed photo of Diana on the wall. Janet sat down with a tin of biscuits and Saul sat down.

"So to what do I owe this honour?"

"It's about Diana. I need to explain something."

"I thought it might be."

"She didn't die, as we were told, she nearly did."

"Oh. I did wonder, please tell me."

Sometime later Janet got up and said, "Yes I never really believed she was dead. I am so happy. I would love to meet her, carry on. Of course I forgive her, and I understand. She was working for the good guys, under cover or something like that. If she won't take Drift back tell her she will have to take at least two of Drift's puppies."

"I'll ask her, or you can."

"When can I see her?"

Three days later a brand-new Land Rover drew up in the farm yard of Janet's farm. She watched it from the feedstore where she was bagging up feed. When she saw Diana get out, she left what she was doing and came out. Diana looked at her and said, "I am sorry, Janet, I really am."

"Well I'm not. Mr Catchpole explained."

"Can I buy a couple of pups from you?"

"No, you can have them. They are registered, eye tested and fit. Out of Biff."

"Thanks, now let me help with that feed. Have you help here?"

"Yes, I've a good farmworker. He's off today."

Diana spent the rest of the day there. Her reunion with Drift was a very happy one, for both of them. Drift insisted on bringing Di to the puppies. Diana said, "She is happy. Look are you busy next Wednesday?"

"No, I don't think so, why?"

"Could I borrow you for the day? I'm having a sort of party a quiet one. I'd like you there, not too posh but respectable."

"Yes, sure what is happening?"

"Just a day out. I'll get a taxi to fetch and bring you back."

"A drinking party. Fine. You are being very mysterious!"

"The other thing is, I need to buy some stock. Not the Suffolks, but have you some Dorsets for sale, lambs I mean?"

"Yes, quite a lot."

"I'd buy them at a proper price. I'll look for an unrelated tup."

"Do you want Kendal Roughs and Mules as well?"

"Yes please."

When Diana got back that evening Saul said, "Come and talk after you have had a bath. You look and smell as you did when I first met you."

Later after a meal, Jake and Di sat down in the lounge. Anna turned off the television and said, "What not out galivanting? Are you perchance running out of steam?"

"No, we wanted to ask you if you would give us a whole day next Wednesday? We need you two."

"Why?"

"We'll tell you then. Will you?"

"Yes, I am sure we can."

When Saul and Anna got up to their bedroom, Saul said, "You know what they are planning, don't you? I think we need to be a step ahead of them."

Chapter Eleven

The case in the juvenile court was short as the three youths admitted their guilt and were placed in a secure youth establishment. No witnesses were called, and Saul was leaving the court building, and walking down one of the passages to the exit when he was confronted by Yvonne Salter-Hicks, who blocked his way and said, "I want a word with you."

"Well I have nothing to say to you. Please let me pass."

Saul looked around and with some relief saw a woman he knew from the Crown Prosecution Service and two magistrates approaching from behind Salter-Hicks. Another magistrate came up behind him and was waiting to pass as well. Salter-Hicks said in a shrill like screech, "I have something to say to you, you will hear it. Isn't it enough that you and your wife robbed Ruth of her inheritance? Then you try to destroy my career. Ruth is locked away because of you, and I may be out of a job and it is all your fault! You are an arrogant, interfering, money grabbing insult to humanity. I hate you, and I will do whatever I can to bring you down. What? Nothing to say? No police chums to hide behind?

Just members of the public who might see you for what you are."

Saul waited for the tirade to finish.

"What kind of man are you? The kind of wimp who rapes women, hides behind his Masonic friends, bullies children, abuses his wife and her sister? I know all about you, you rapist."

Saul could hear hurried movement behind him. He looked towards her and waited.

"Not got any reply? Typical man lost for words because someone tells the truth about you. I hate you for what you are, and what you've done."

She lunged at him and swung her arm that had been behind her, towards him and hit Saul very hard with something that was long, black and wooden. Saul felt the sting as blood began to pour from a cut on his temple. It started to run into his eye. He felt very strange and stepped back, aware of someone behind him, and said, "This is neither the time or the place for arguments or fighting. Your comments are not worthy of a reply. I have nothing to say to you, let me pass."

As Yvonne went to hit him again, he was pushed aside by a court usher and a uniformed policeman, followed by a WPC. Saul reached into his pocket and pulled out a clean handkerchief and held it to his head, and then looked at the blood on it.

One of the magistrates came and supported him and said to the uniformed officers, "Arrest that woman and hold on to her. Bring her before me in half an hour. Mr Catchpole, come with me, you've gone a rather pale colour. Let's have a look at you."

Saul nodded to the PC and turned and followed the magistrate and his lady colleague and was taken into the magistrate's room and pushed into a chair.

"Sit down and let me see. Yes, that needs attention."

"Thank you, Dr Hebden, isn't it? I'll be all right, it's just a scratch."

"No, it isn't, it will need stitching, I think. We heard it all. Will you tell us what this is all about? Was it someone you have dealt with in the past?"

"No, I am afraid it is personal. She is the lesbian lover of my sister-in-law, who made a similar scene at my home recently. This woman has previously made a complaint against me about a case that has just been in Juvenile court, I think you were on the bench. Mrs Morrison, isn't it?"

"Yes, that right. Look write all this down. Gerry. Have you called an ambulance?"

The court usher replied, "Yes, ma'am, I have. It is on its way."

"Doctor, can't you stich it? I must go and finish some work."

Dr Hebden said, "Well I suppose I could if I were not a doctor of mathematics, not medicine. The only place you are going is casualty. What did she hit you with?"

"I don't know, something wooden."

Gerry said, "I saw it, sir, it was one of them very heavy sort of round rulers what they use in technical drawing offices."

"Nasty. She could have had your eye out. You were very restrained, and did not retaliate at all? Why?"

"No point, your worship. I was getting ready to disarm her. I don't hit women, despite what she said."

"Well we will all give evidence if required."

"I don't think I am any of the things she alleges. I may be a bit arrogant at times, but I was not aware I was a child bullier!"

"Of course you aren't. and you are not a Mason either. I would know because I am one. Usher please send the medics in here and stay here with Mr Catchpole until they arrive."

"Yes, sir. They have arrested her, and she is down in the cells now. Here, Mr Catchpole, I've put your briefcase here beside you. You have gone ever so pale. Are you all right?"

"No, Gerry, I think I am going to be sick."

"Well come through here into the cloakroom. Now it's my turn to come to your aid, like you did with me a couple of years back."

Saul was very relieved he had made it to the toilet before he was sick and felt a bit better for it. His head was swimming and he was sweating. Gerry never left his side, persuading Saul to lay down on a couch.

"I remember, there was a fight in the public gallery. They set about you when you asked them to leave. I just happened to be there."

"Yes, and thanks to you I wasn't badly hurt. Now lie quiet and we'll soon have you off to casualty."

The ambulance crew came very quickly and put him onto a trolley and then whisked him away in the ambulance. Saul was sick several more times. Before long he was feeling slightly less nauseous and a doctor came into the cubicle. "What, you again? Not been flying off any cliffs this time? Lie down and let me have a look at you."

"No this was just a woman with a perceived grudge."

"Quite a grudge! I am sending you down to X-ray and it will need four or five stitches. I trust you are not planning on entering any beauty contests in the next few days. You are going to have a splendid black eye."

The doctor looked into his eyes and Saul muttered, "Oh no. I'm meant to be at my brother's wedding the day after tomorrow."

"If you are well enough, I'll let you out for it."

"I can't stay in, I'm due in court this afternoon."

"Tough. We will see what the X-ray shows. You have had a nasty crack across the temple. Not a place to take risks with. Nurse send him down to X-ray please, on a trolley until we are sure. I don't want you walking anywhere."

While waiting outside X-ray Alan materialized beside him. "It's all right, I sorted the court out. Jake is bringing Anna in with some things for you. Everything is under control."

"Thanks, can you take my briefcase back with you?"

"Yes and your suit to the cleaners as soon as you have changed. You are going to have some shiner. I hope Jake and Di appreciate it on Wednesday!"

"Are you coming, then?"

"Yes, but you don't know that yet. What can I do for you?"

"Get me out of here?"

"No way. I can, however, deputize for you in court, it's only antecedents, isn't it? They are in your case?" Do you want me to bring anything in for you?"

"A good book to read if you won't spring me."

"Stevenson?"

"NO, thank you. I am afraid I am going to chuck up again. Can you call the nurse?"

Half an hour later Saul was wheeled back to casualty and the doctor saw him again. "Fortunately, no fracture but I want you kept in for observations tonight and if you are better you can go in the morning. Now the nurse will stitch you."

Saul was quite grateful to be left in peace once he had been treated. When he woke Anna was beside him. He felt much better and sat up without feeling giddy. Having assured her he was well looked after he drifted back to sleep.

He was released the next day and spent it quietly at home. The following morning a taxi called for him and the family, and Jake, and took them to a large and rather splendid hotel. All his four children were there as well as Alan and a couple of longstanding family friends.

Jake cleared his throat and said, "I asked you to come and watch me and Diana get hitched, at the registry office just down the road and we want you to be witnesses. It is an easy walk, shall we go?"

No one was very surprised. A happy party walked down the street. Once there the registrar came out and spoke to them, and Saul recognized her as one of the operatic society. Diana arrived with Janet and they went in.

The ceremony was short and sweet. There were no frills, and the party walked back to the hotel where they all had a delicious buffet lunch. Then it was Saul's turn to surprise Jake, and presents were duly given, and toasts and speeches made. At the party Diana said to Saul, "We didn't fool you for a moment. I've bought the farm next to Jake and we will combine the two. I have employed a shepherd, who you also know, Nick. We're off to Wales for a short holiday. We'll see you when we get back. I understand you were hit with a pole of some sort. Surely you should be catching poles, not stopping them?"

"Thank you so much for that gem! Now go and have wonderful time."

***

Simon Hobbs didn't like prison very much. His arrogance made him enemies very quickly. He decided he needed to do something about it. He spent a lot of time in the prison library. His defence solicitor had explained to him the mass of evidence piling up against him. He wasn't sure he wanted to leave his freedom to a jury. Cantone had been very inconvenient with what he had said, and what he was undoubtedly going to say. He made several phone calls and then asked for a visiting order.

Christopher Dodds was a drunk and a hopeless alcoholic. He saw very little future for himself, caught in an endless spiral of drunkenness, living by whatever means he could, coming home to a dismal room, in a sad and dirty guesthouse. He received his brother's offer with interest. Prison was not unknown to him and he decided it was better than his current life. If the plan worked, he could look forward to a change for the better. The money he had been sent was enough to clean himself up and to sustain his needs for a week or so. He caught the train to Wakefield and went to visit his brother in the prison there.

Tom Cantone had accepted his new routine in prison. He was a model prisoner. He was rather looking forward to the trial, when he could produce his finest performance. At night, in his cell he would rehearse what he was going to say, and how he would say it.

Anita was desperately unhappy. She missed the company of a man, and the comforts that money could give. She had been advised by her solicitor and was dreading the trial. She was worried the jury would see through her and find her guilty. Of murder. He solicitor had been quite frank about the chances.

The prison discovered Hobbs' escape after three days. Dobbs had started suffering the effects of alcohol withdrawal and had been examined by the prison doctor who had noticed several discrepancies. He had spotted that Dobbs, although looking very like Hobbs, did not have an appendix scar, which he had previously recorded. When questioned, Dobbs admitted swapping with his twin brother, and explained that this was not the first time they had pulled this trick.

Paul was in the office when he received the message of the escape. Initial enquires had revealed nothing of any use. Hobbs had, effectively, disappeared. He rang Saul.

Saul came into work still sporting black eyes, and Alan was moments behind him. The three of them talked it through. Alan explained that the mother had suggested that Simon was in prison, and no one had thought to follow it up. Paul told them he had asked the local force to visit the mother and get more information. He had also asked the same of Stoke on Trent and of the officers in Rotherham.

"It looks like we have been well and truly had, sir, now what? I've also been in touch with Charlie and got a number for a mobile that Hobbs may have had. I am getting the phone company to find out if it has pinged off masts recently and if so, where, and more importantly where it is now."

"When we searched the flat, did we find anything that might now head us in the right direction, think back? You saw a lot, Paul, will you go back and look please? Alan ring the prison where Cantone is, and warn them."

"The Essex police are searching the dump that Dobbs was living in. We already have details of Hobbs' bank accounts and cards, and he will need money if he is on the run, but I doubt he will be that easy to find. I'll get any transactions monitored."

At Hobbs' flat little had changed since their previous visit. Charlie had obviously taken his things, but the place still reeked of stale perfume. Saul let the other officers look round and sat down in the lounge and thought about it. He tried to remember exactly what the room had been like when he had been there. He noticed that the Louis XIV chair was missing, the one he had been asked not to sit in. Then on the marble topped table he looked for the cigarette lighter and a holder that had been there. They were also missing. He got up and began to look around very carefully, He jotted down a list of things that he thought were missing. Several paintings were gone, good ones. There was also some ornate Satsuma wear missing. Then he missed several art deco statuettes.

"Paul, Alan, did we photograph in here, when we searched it?"

"I'll check, why?"

"There is a lot missing, a lot of the more valuable things. That cigarette holder he said was Noel Coward's, for a start."

"Yes, I remember, and the chair, where has that gone? I'll check if anything like that is in any of the other rooms. Were any of the photographs submitted as evidence?"

"No so hopefully he will not think we will miss anything. How would he be able to sell things like that?"

"Dealers, auction markets, sales, things like that."

"Check them. Start with the big ones: Christie's, Sotheby's, Bonhams. See what has gone and what is going to go through. Paul, see Charlie and find out anything to help us. I will contact the prison to see who he talked to, who he wrote to, and who he made calls to. Did we not take fingerprints in here?"

"Yes, we did. Do we need to do it again, to see if anyone else has been in?"

"It won't hurt. I'll talk to the landlord and the neighbours. There is already an all ports warning out on him. We still have his passport, but I am sure he has others. I'll go and see the lady in the sari shop opposite, she watches everything. I suppose he will change his appearance."

"Yes, and remember, he's an actor, he's very good at it. I expect the beard will have gone. Did you notice any wigs anywhere?"

"Yes, there are some in one of the bedrooms and also there seem to be a few missing, as there are gaps in the display."

It took them two days to follow up their initial enquiries. On the third day, Geoff was sitting at the desk when they came in. After greeting him, Saul said, "It's great to see you but if you need more time, you can take it, you know."

"Actually, sir, I think I may be able to help."

"How?"

"Simon was a talkative man. He liked to impress. I mentioned once that I had been to a show at Rhyl. He always tried to say he 'd been to one better or posher, or he had done it before. You know, you had an elephant, he had a bag to put it in. You had a black cat, he had one blacker. He mentioned he knew Rhyl rather well. Said he had some good friends there, fellow thespians. I don't know Rhyl that well, but he does."

"He didn't say who or where, did he?"

"No, but he mentioned a place two miles out from town. Said it was sort of an artiste's refuge. From what he said I sort of got the impression it was a hippy type community. He did say it was a magnificent very old mansion, once owned by an industrialist, a patron of the arts, who had left it to a group, as a refuge. He did mention it had a swimming pool, a small theatre and the gardens were massive. I was thinking, there can't be too many places like that. So I rang Rhyl two days ago as soon as I heard he had escaped, and they are checking now."

"Well done, anything else you can think of?"

"He also boasted that he never flew and went everywhere in his car. I happen to know it is an old Morris Oxford. I even know the number. He wrecked it by re-doing the interior in shocking pink. The number is CUT1E. I've circulated that too. He kept it garaged, two streets from his flat."

"Anything else?",

"Well nothing concrete, it's just…"

"Just what?"

"Something I saw, ages ago. It may be nothing, but it has been bugging me. As well as his live-in man friend, Charlie, he was chatting up Maurice Fabre, to no avail, but I didn't think that was who he was really interested in. I think he was trying to make someone jealous."

"Who?"

"I don't know, for sure. I once saw Simon and young Aloysius Baker, at a wine bar on the far side of town, in what seemed a very clandestine meeting. They didn't see me. I was on an enquiry for another case. I was in the back, talking to the manager when they came in separately. I was watching them. The manager told me they were regulars. That was ages ago."

"Flavia's son? I know he is gay. Get his prints checked against anything found at the flat. Find him, not you, Geoff, get someone else to."

"I will, sir. Who's been knocking you around?"

"My sister-in-law's lesbian lover!"

"Should you be back at work, it must have been quite a blow?"

"It was. Knocked me silly for a while. I totally disgraced myself by chucking up in the magistrates' private toilet, and again at the hospital. The doctor told me I was not to fight for a while!"

"Like you do so much fighting? I hope she looks worse than you do."

"I never touched her. She bit one poor officer, and spat at the magistrate, Dr Hebden, who didn't take kindly to that at all!"

"Yes I know Bill Hebden. He wouldn't!"

PC Gethyn Evans, a long serving officer at Rhyl, knew the place they were looking for. He called there with some other officers but drew a blank. Something was worrying him, however, and he decided to look a little closer. After some thought he rang Saul. "I am sorry to bother you, sir, you know we went out to the Manor to check, like, for your man on the run?"

"Yes, anything come up?"

"Well yes and no, sir. We were invited in to search, which we did, but it has been bugging me. You see I used to go there as a lad, played in the grounds with the head gardener's son. I've been trying to remember. We used to play in an old tunnel. Brick it were, it was used as a wine cellar, or some of it was. There were a passage at the back, like, what was kept locked, but I think it went through to the house. Now when we searched there was no trace of that old tunnel, just hillside, but there were no hill there when I was a lad, just the tunnel. Anyway, I rang my old playmate up and asked him if the tunnel had been pulled down, and he said, no, they had covered it over with a small earthwork like thing. Now I had a look from the other side of the valley, with a set of binoculars. There was the hill, and I noticed a concrete path just leading straight into the hill. The flower beds have been newly planted up, since we was there two days ago. Daft really, 'cos what is planted there won't survive that close to the rhododendrons."

"Go on."

"Well, when I was a kid there was a story that the manor had several secret rooms and passages, but me and my chum never found them. I wondered if that is where the cellar passage went."

"You think this man Hobbs is there?"

"Well he could be, and well, I've always found them a right funny lot, all arty crafty and a bit hippy like. Can't say I took to them and I thought I should tell you. I hope I'm not wasting your time?"

"Far from it, thank you. Could you keep watching and find someone to get a search warrant for me? Was this tunnel large enough to hide a car in?"

"Several of them yes, they grew mushrooms in it at one time."

"Right, I will ring your station and officially ask for help. Do you have a local auction house?"

"To be sure we do, Morgan, Davies and Gwilt. I'll get the number for you. I happen to know they are having a big sale next Monday. Funny you should ask that. I saw one of their vans coming away from the Manor yesterday. They put their sales online, you can look up and see what is going for sale. I know because I regularly check it for stolen items."

As Saul was organizing the new line of enquiry, he came into the squad room and Nita said, "Young Baker has done a bunk. His mother is frantic with worry. We checked and not only has he been in Hobbs' flat recently, he and another chap were seen moving things out, mainly in large boxes. No one thought much of it as he was a frequent visitor there. Meanwhile, Dobbs has said he has no idea where Hobbs is, but he has been rather talkative about their rather confused and interesting pasts. It is not the first time he has served a sentence for his brother. Now Charlie has been seen and he says it is quite possible Hobbs is at Rhyl, and he thought that Hobbs was at least a part owner of the place although he never let Charlie go there."

"The plot thickens! It looks like we need a team to go to Rhyl. I have just been in touch with their Superintendent who will find us accommodation if needed and will happily help us. They have long been a bit uneasy about the Manor, convinced amongst other things that they are cultivating cannabis, but have never managed to find it on several raids. He did tell me that the electricity bill is suspiciously low. The electric provider came to see him and said they had no electricity used for several months, but there are always lots of lights on. He made enquiries and there are no generators. It is likely they are abstracting the electric. He actually has a warrant ready to search but will get another by the time we can get there, to include vehicles and anything else we may be looking for. Now, Geoff, please will you take charge here, and I need a team to join me in a trip to Wales. Bring overnight gear and I want you ready to go in an hour!"

They arrived in Rhyl and took up positions by six that evening. Saul with the local superintendent, went to the front door armed with several warrants. PC Evans took Paul and Nita (who had insisted she wanted to come) and some uniform officers to the rear of the main house, where the tunnel had once been. Other officers were covering all the known exits to the house and to the grounds.

The front door was answered, and the warrants were shown to the older of the two men who answered the door.

Saul said, "We intend to do a complete and thorough search, including in the old tunnel. If necessary, we will pull the place apart. Do you want to save us time and effort and show me the hidden rooms and passages that we know are here?"

The man looked rather startled and stared at him. A younger man moved casually over to a desk in the hallway and before anyone could stop him, he pressed something underneath it. When they looked it was an alarm button. Superintendent Collins said, "Thank you. We have the place surrounded, and anyone trying to leave will be apprehended. Officers arrest these two for obstruction and take them away to the vans outside. Search them and bring me any phones they may have, and any keys."

The older man said, "No, wait, Quentin, you fool! They obviously know he and his chum are here. Let's not make it worse for ourselves. We are in enough trouble already. All right I will show you."

The teams started searching and then Saul went with the older man through the house to a panelled landing on the third floor, where a panel slid back to reveal some stairs going down. At the bottom was a door. The man handed Saul a key and said, "Down there."

Saul looked at him and said, "After you."

The man shook his head and said, "No I'm not going down there. I don't know the code. If you don't get it right it opens a trap door."

"Into which you hoped I would fall. Charming! Get any other keys he has and then take him away. Move back everyone, to the end of the landing. Two of you, please wait just behind this corner and let us know if there is any movement. Let anyone come out, and then we can trap them. Before you go, do you want to tell us any other nasty little traps? If not, as you said you are already in trouble. Don't make it worse for yourself."

The man shook his head and was led away.

The alarm bell in the small secret room made Simon Hobbs sit up with a start. He went to look at some television screens on the wall.

Aloysius said, "What is it?"

"They are all around the house. Another raid. They might just be checking. I expect Charlie has been talking. They were here a couple of days ago, making enquiries after me. We can't get out of any of the usual doors, so we will have to get out through the tunnel as a last resort. Stop blubbing, you fool! Now, plan C. Put on the female costume, and I'll put on my dress. We'll make ourselves up. They are looking for two chaps, not women. We'll be able to fool them; they don't know either of us. They won't find us for ages, there are too many precautions laid down. Remember what I told you to do. It looks like it's just the local fuzz. They may just be on yet another of their fruitless drugs raids."

Dressed and made up as women they prepared to escape. Simon flounced down the rickety stairs, unlocked the door to the tunnel and looked into the blackness. He found a torch on a hook by the door and crept forward and opened his car door and took out a small case. He paused beside a small pile of things and thoughtfully put a small cigarette holder in the pocket of his dress. He returned back to the secret room with the case and put the contents into a handbag which he had in his hand, and said, "Right we go out of the third panel and into one of the large studios. Don't try to get out of the house, it won't work. Say nothing. You just go down to the kitchens and join the others there. They will pretend you are one of them. I know I can fool these local coppers, and when they have gone and found nothing, as usual, we'll sneak away. If they do unlock the door, the trap will open and the stairs collapse, and any coppers will go down into the cellar, and they will be so busy rescuing them they will call in anyone outside to help them. Then we can go out of the tunnel in the car and be well away before they can catch us. If you cry, dearest, you will make your make-up run. I will look after you."

PC Evans and Nita hunted around the area where a well-worn path abruptly stopped at a grass bank at the top of a large lawned mound. She looked carefully at a small and old tree stump nearby and pulled on a small branch on it. Nothing happened. She pushed the branch and heard an electric motor start up almost under her feet. She let go of the branch and looked round. Paul, who had been nearby said, "Do that again. Keep going, I think something moved."

Nita pushed the trunk right down and the motor started again, and they watched, with several other officers as the hillside seemed to fold in on itself and a huge brick tunnel was revealed. The smell of cannabis was almost overwhelming. Just inside the tunnel entrance, facing outwards, was an old Morris Oxford with the number plate, CUT1E. Once the motor had stopped, they cautiously entered the tunnel.

Paul looked around and said, "Nita, please go back with one of these officers to the trunk. If we go in, I do not want us trapped in there."

At the back of the tunnel, having passed the large cannabis growing area, they found a locked door. It was old and very heavy. It was designed to open towards them, and it was too big to force. They called up to other members of the searching squad to see if any keys had been found. After a few minutes another officer arrived with a massive bunch of keys, some of which looked very old. Eventually they found one that fitted the door. As they turned the key in an obviously newly oiled lock the outside door began to close on them. Nita and her companion quickly reactivated the motor and the doors reopened.

Simon heard men at the bottom of the steps and he and Aloysius left hurriedly through the other door. They could see no one on any of the steps. Simon keyed in a code to a panel on the wall, and they softly crept up the steps and listened. They heard nothing, so Simon quietly opened the panel and looked out in the large corridor on the third floor. They listened for several minutes but, hearing nothing, they came out, shut the panel and turned towards the main landing. As they turned the corner to the head of the stairs, they came face to face with Saul, and half a dozen uniformed officers.

Simon, in a very realistic high-pitched voice, said, "Oh my goodness you startled me. Whatever is going on? I was asleep in my room and I thought I heard something and so I called Lucinda here in the next room and we came out to see what it was."

He looked behind him to see several other police officers approaching. Saul had to admit that Hobbs made a very convincing woman, and with a rather sly smile said, "Good disguise, Hobbs, I'll give you that.

Not good enough, however. You are both under arrest. You, Barker, go with these officers now. Hobbs come with me. Saul reached forwards and pulled off the wig Hobbs was wearing. Hobbs sighed and said in his normal voice, "You really don't like me much, do you Mr Senior Policeman?"

"Not much, no. I doubt a jury will either. Take him away, search him, caution him and then get him into a safe custody centre."

Hobbs looked up into Saul's face and pointed to the cut and stitches above his temple. "I hope that hurt rather a lot. Who did it, I would like to shake their hand?"

"No, you wouldn't, not your type at all, duckie."

"Oh a woman. I quite like them too."

"Not this sort, she wouldn't like you."

"Oh well, please tell her I wish it had been me."

"I am sure you do. Get this prisoner out of my sight please."

**

Saul and his team from Yorkshire were busy for the rest of the evening, with statements and exhibits that had been taken. They assisted the team from Rhyl with the enormous number of things found at the Manor. At about ten thirty they went to their accommodation in one of the hotels and returned the next morning to continue with the many tasks that needed to be done. Saul and Nita went, with PC Jones, to the auction house, and identified many items that had belonged to Hobbs. These were then checked against a list of stolen property and most of them were found to be stolen and were duly seized. Aloysius Baker went totally to pieces and admitted assisting Hobbs and then taking the Morris Oxford to Huddersfield railway station to collect Hobbs and then travelling to Rhyl. A check revealed that Aloysius Baker did not have any type of driving licence. The team were kept busy all day and, in the evening, they were invited to a drink at a public house as a mark of gratitude from the local officers. Saul knew it was a bad idea when they moved on to a nightclub. Their Welsh colleagues were most hospitable. Saul decided it was time to let them relax.

The next morning he went down to breakfast. He was the only one. Gradually the team came downstairs in a very sorry state. Alan looked almost green and only drank black coffee. Nita tried to toy with a croissant but failed. Paul announced he was sure he was unfit to drive, and several others agreed that they were in a similar state. Saul had little option but to extend their stay but explained that they would not be getting this on expenses. They readily agreed with this. At lunch time

Saul announced they were all going on an invigorating walk by the sea. Nita groaned, "Must we?"

Alan leaned over and said, "I've been warned about this and his 'suggestions'. I think we must, Nita. It's his way of teaching us a lesson. It isn't a bad thought though; it might make us feel a bit better."

Paul said, "Just how far were you considering going, sir? Alan is right, but not too far, I beg of you."

Saul grinned. "We'll see how far we get. Meet in the lobby in fifteen minutes, everyone."

Saul allowed himself a quiet chuckle when they set off. It was a cold and blustery day and to keep warm they had to walk briskly. Saul rather enjoyed himself.

Nita caught up with him. "Sir, take pity, please! I am not a walking person!"

"You are now. Where have Alan and Caroline gone?"

"They dropped behind some way back. They seem to get on very well together."

"Yes, I had noticed that too. Then we will wait for all of us to catch up."

Alan and Caroline looked a bit sheepish when they finally caught up with the group. Saul looked at the nearby café, and said, "In there, all of you. I'll stand you all a nice hot invigorating drink, no not an alcoholic one."

They were the only ones in the café and sat supping hot drinks which soon became a lunch. The walk back was much more cheerful. Saul rather annoyingly was still chuckling when they got back to the hotel. Alan joined him in the lounge. "I'm sorry, Saul, I should have known better. I'm not really a drinker. I got a bit out of my depth."

"You and the rest of the crew. Is there something you want to tell me?"

"Yes, I asked Caroline to marry me this afternoon. She said yes. How on earth did you know?"

"It wasn't hard to work out. It was only a matter of time. I am so happy for you both."

Saul, when the time comes, will you be my best man?"

"I'd be delighted to, Alan."

Chapter Twelve

Months later, Cantone gave his evidence at the trial, very well. He was convincing, candid and almost came across as being easily led, and gullible, quite the love smitten fool. It was an excellent performance. Hobbs' counsel tried to pull his evidence apart, and even succeeded on a couple of points, but Saul wondered just what the jury would make of it.

Anita went totally to pieces, and almost convicted herself. She had insisted on giving her side of it, against her counsel's advice. She was caught out in many lies, and with the weight of evidence against her she came across as mercenary, shallow and manipulative.

Hobbs was quite a different matter. His was a polished performance being confident but not overly so, and almost convincing. His defence counsel had kept Saul in the witness box for three days, but Saul had patiently kept his cool and hoped he and Alan had convinced the court of Hobbs' guilt. The judge gave a very impartial summing up.

Saul waited while the jury went out. As Cantone had pleaded guilty it was only the verdicts of Anita and Hobbs that were being decided. They retired on the

Friday and were out for the Monday and it was only on the Tuesday that he was called back into court to hear their verdicts. As the jury came back in, you could have heard a pin drop.

"On the charge of murder, how do you find the defendant, Simon Hobbs?"

"Guilty."

"And is that the verdict of you all?"

"Yes, it is."

"And on the charge of murder, how do you find Anita Jones? Guilty or not guilty?"

"Guilty."

"Is that the verdict of you all?"

"Yes, it is."

Saul hadn't realized he'd been holding his breath but let it out almost as a sigh of relief. All three defendants got the expected life sentences. He finished up at court and went back to his office. The ACC from Derbyshire was in his office waiting for him. "Congratulations, Catchpole. I heard the verdict. I have a result for you too. Sit down please. Now the complaint against you by Salter-Hicks has been proved unfounded, and malicious. You are exonerated, totally."

"Thank you, sir."

"As you know your sister-in-law, Ruth Hughes has been declared unfit to plead and is detained in a mental hospital. I have investigated all her allegations about you, and others and her complaints against Withers and every other officer she had dealings with, and those made by Salter-Hicks after her assault on you. What I do not think you knew, and I am now telling you is, after I had a long conversation with the retired Chief Superintendent Duff, I started a very close look at the deaths of your father-in-law and mother-in-law, and of a Lady Matilda Agatha Sacree. This was at the request of your Chief Constable and endorsed by my Chief and your Police Authority. It opened up a very nasty can of worms. Although I cannot prove it, I suspect that Ruth Hughes tampered with the brakes on her father's car, and that caused the crash in which he and his wife died. That will remain on file. What we can prove, however, is that she killed Lady Sacree. For this we had to do an exhumation and found a lethal high dose of digitalis in her body, the same as we found in Ruth's possessions. There was also a sedative present and this we found, not under any prescription, in the property of Salter-Hicks. It became very apparent that they planned it together, and so Salter-Hicks was interviewed and eventually admitted her part in it, and that she supplied the sedative. She is fit to plead and comes up for sentence for that and her assault on you, next week. We thought it was best you were in no way involved or even aware of what we were doing. Now, I have spoken to your delightful wife and explained everything. She understands and is happy with what we have done. You will not be needed at court unless you wish to be there."

"I was not looking forward to giving evidence about it I must admit."

"So far as I understand you behaved impeccably and with great restraint. It has left a bit of a scar. Is it all healed? No problems, headaches, dizzy spells?"

"None, I have what my brother describes a thick skull."

"Yes, I rather liked him, and his wife. I went out to their farm, saw them there. She reminds me of a very clever officer I worked with long ago in Wiltshire. It can't be her, because I was told she had died. That woman could do *The Times* crossword in just a few minutes and was the only woman who ever beat me at chess, the only person in fact. Now according to Lady Matilda's will, if Ruth Hughes cannot inherit, which she is now unable to do, you receive her share of the inheritance."

"My wife, surely"

"NO, you, personally. She was most definite in her instructions when making her will. I know you have correctly declared all your private means to the relevant persons, as is only proper, but may I be very nosy and ask if you have plans for the money?"

"Well I don't want that huge house, certainly, but it cannot be used as a house of multiple occupancy, so I will have to sell it. I will put the money to a charity that Matilda wanted me to set up."

"Her solicitor told me all about that. Her specific instructions were that Ruth must not use it for that purpose, but you can do as you like with it. The solicitor thought it might make a wonderful shelter for families that need a safe haven, and for helping youngsters that might not ever get a good chance in life through no fault of their own."

"That changes things, yes it would."

"I trust you have no hard feelings against me over all this?"

"You were only doing your job, I know that. I thank you for the diligence with which you have pursued it. No, no hard feelings."

"That is quite a relief. I can now tell you that you are the most stiff backed, prickly and pedantic officer I've ever investigated. You are so correct and precise it put me through hoops. Long may you remain so. I wish every officer was as straight as you. I was due to retire three months ago and only hung on to finish this case. I am moving to Skipton, not far away. I doubt we will meet again, but if you could stand it, I would rather like to help with this charity."

"Really, how much could you help?"

"As much as you want me too. I have to do something. I had a son with what can only be described as a learning disability. Nothing bad, but he could best be described as slow. He also had a heart condition and died a few years ago. If his problems had been spotted earlier and he had had help sooner, he might have realized what potential he had. His passion was gardening, but no one would take him on because he was not very literate. Before I joined Wiltshire, I was an accountant you know. Need any help in the treasurer's department?"

"Need it, Mr Brewer, we are desperately looking for a treasurer. Paid, of course and a trustee. Would you consider it?"

"Yes, Saul, I would. Give me something worthwhile to do. I don't play golf, don't play cards and don't want to be stuck at home all the time. My wife passed on two years ago. It's Con, short for Constantine."

They shook hands and he left.

Shortly after the squad was called out to another suspected murder and were busy with that.

***

Saul and a lot of his team took their seats in the theatre. His sons, Samuel and Stephen and his daughter Susan sat between him and Anna. He relaxed as the overture began. He rather liked Patience. His daughter Sharon was one of the chorus in the show. When Jake came on as a foppish poet, he began to laugh. His sergeants, Julia Pellow and Geoff Bickerstaff, both had principal roles. It hardly seemed nine months since the last production. Saul really enjoyed the operetta.

Afterwards, in the Green Room, Flavia came over to him. "The sets you painted for us are wonderful. Thank you so much. I also want to thank you for everything you did, not just for the society, but what you said in Aloysius' mitigation. He is doing well you know now, gone into hairdressing. I accept it and what he is. Thank you for your discretion. You kept your word."

"I always try to. This was a splendid production, didn't recognize Bunthorne. Is he new?"

"Yes, we have several, your daughter shows promise. Did you say you didn't sing? What a pity, we can always use more men. Your brother will I think be a splendid Sir Despard in Ruddigore next summer. His wife, she won't go on stage, but she is a brilliant make-up artist."

"Yes she is good. Believe me, you do not want me singing. Jake is the musical one in my family."

"Yes, we never stop laughing when he is around. Are you coming to the party next week?"

"I think the whole family is."

The next day, Saul decided the office was looking untidy. He announced a cleanup, as most of the team were in and there were no urgent cases on. He started in his office while the main office was the task of the squad. Alan was helping as his office was already immaculately tidy. As Saul cleared out and filed some of the case files, he came across a charter, which he decided needed to be framed.

He paused to read it.

The Murder Squad Walking Society
President: C/Supt Catchpole
Vice President: DI Withers
Secretary: WDC Nita Kaur

There followed a list of all the officers who had been to Rhyl.

Honorary Member: PC Gethyn Evans, Rhyl Police Station

The society shall be known as the Murder Squad Walking Society. Membership, when allocated, is compulsory.

Rules

1) The Squad members shall be required to be away from their home station.
2) A liberal amount of alcohol must be consumed.
3) Participants must feel jaded, hungover or ill to compete.
4) The weather must be cold and wet.
5) There must be at least one courting couple in attendance.
6) The leader will be C/Supt Catchpole, who will determine the route, and ensure the completion of it by all entrants.
7) The leader will provide suitable refreshment during the march.
8) There will be no arguments and no resignations.
9) Membership is compulsory for life. All members will wear the society insignia when on parade.
10) Punishment for not participating will be gimlet eyes and a heavy frown.
11) Membership is only open to members of the Murder Squad or those on attachment to it.
12) Reunions are at the discretion of the President.

Saul looked down at his tie pin, that he wore with some pride It depicted a leek and waves on a shore. Around its border was TMSWS – President.

The End